Cavan studied Holt. "Only one man dies today," he declared. "Is this not a pretty day for a gunfight?"

Holt worked to tamp down his fear as he faced Cavan. "You will do it?" he said. "You will let the cattle drive proceed?"

"I gave my word." Cavan's head hovered above his gun butt. "As I gave my word to kill you and have your woman." Cavan approached to within five paces. "Enough talk. Slap leather."

Holt did, before the sentence was complete—and saw in an eyeblink what was about to happen. He dropped toward the snow as his barrel cleared the holster.

Cavan shot him.

GOD'S COUNTRY

Steven M. Krauzer

FAWCETT GOLD MEDAL • NEW YORK

A Fawcett Gold Medal
Published by Ballantine Books
Copyright © 1993 by Steven M. Krauzer

Library of Congress Catalog Card Number: 93-90528

ISBN 0-449-14868-8

Manufactured in the United States of America

First Edition: November 1993

CHAPTER ONE

Holt wiped sweat from his eye sockets and blinked at Doare and Morano as they crossed the yard. Beside him, Billy Card muttered, "What do they want?" But he knew the answer as well as Holt.

The two thugs wanted to knock Holt's teeth down his throat, then break his arm for mumbling.

Doare wasn't any taller than Holt, maybe six feet, but the muscles of his arms and torso were ropy and knotted. He had a set of barbells and he used them daily. Morano was simply the biggest Mexican Holt had ever seen, a huge ball of brown flesh six and a half feet long and four wide atop thick, too-short bandy legs. Morano wore boots, against regulations; Doare's barbells were also against regulations, but rules didn't apply to Doare and Morano.

At noon of an August day the sun blasted down on the expanse of hard-packed dirt, empty of any object offering the most remote sliver of shade. Bare-chested men grouped in huddles, shuffled aimlessly, smoked cigarettes, dreamed stuporous heat-fever dreams. Forty-foot-high granite-block walls enclosed three sides of the yard; on the fourth, under a veranda, six warders sat rocking their chairs back on two legs, shotguns cradled on their laps, watching Doare and Morano amble in Holt's direction. Doare was limping. The shotgun guards showed broad grins and no intention of interfering.

Men were starting to get a whiff of something imminent, and Holt felt eyes on him. Little Billy Card moved away to squat on his haunches, wearing a miserable, sorry expression. Holt shrugged: *It couldn't have been helped.*

Billy and Holt had shared a six-by-nine cell for nearly a year now. Billy arranged the transfer after they'd become pals; though he didn't have the pull of Doare and Morano, Billy had a knack for working the system. One of his scams was the photograph business: A couple weeks earlier, Billy had somehow gotten his hands on several dozen copies of an old tintype of a big-breasted dark-haired woman wearing bloomers and nothing else. Eight had already sold, each for five pouches of tobacco or two mason jars of pruno, the hootch that Doare and Morano's gang brewed up in a still in the kitchen's storage closet. The price was fairly dear, but in the Arizona Territorial Prison, pictures of a near-naked woman enjoyed a seller's market.

The previous evening after lockdown, a warder had come to their cells, turned the key, and wandered down the tier, whistling. Billy said, "Aw shit," and shrank back against the far wall beside the toilet. A minute later Doare pushed through the door, extended one of his big mitts palm up, and said, "Gimme." Behind him, Morano lounged against the jamb.

To that point Holt had managed to stay out of the way of the prison boss and his partner Morano, and at the moment he preferred to continue to keep his distance. He'd been building a cigarette when the guard appeared, and now he licked the paper and rolled it closed. He held it out and said to Doare, "Smoke?"

Doare looked at him as if surprised to find a third party in the cell's confines. Doare plucked the cigarette from Holt, examined it briefly, and shredded it between thumb and forefinger.

"I'm trying to give them up myself," Holt said.

Doare jerked a thumb over his shoulder. "Go somewhere." Without waiting to see whether Holt did as he was told, Doare advanced on Billy, who had recovered his wits enough to pretend to lose them.

"What goes on?" he said.

"Gimme them pitchers," Doare said. "I am the mercantilist in this hoosegow."

"Pitchers?" Billy echoed.

"Them pitcures of the nekkid girl."

"Little pitchers have big ears," Billy babbled earnestly.

Doare looked back at Holt, as if he'd forgotten he'd ordered him to leave. "He really a moron?"

"Yup," Holt said pleasantly.

Doare smiled and casually backhanded Billy across the face. Billy slumped to the floor and covered his head with his arms. "Okay," Doare said to Holt, "you tell me where they are."

Doare jerked the thin mattress of the lower bunk onto the floor, revealing the planking underneath. Holt kept his expression neutral, though he knew that Doare wasn't going to find the photos. When Billy had come into their possession, he'd used a spoon, stolen from the mess hall and honed against the cell's wall, to work out the mortar between two of the granite stones, forming a slot just large enough to hold them. It was mudded over with bread soaked in coffee, and the way the coffee was in this place, the dried bread was indistinguishable from cement.

Still, Holt considered telling Doare what he wanted to know; dirty pictures didn't seem a sufficient reason for a ruckus. But he hadn't started this, and if he gave in, it would likely be the first step down a path of continuing trouble.

Besides, he'd been jerked around too much recently. So he smiled back at Doare and said, "I reckon I won't."

Doare bent over, pried up one of Billy's arms with one hand, and punched him in the face with the other. Billy's nose began to bleed. Doare straightened and said to Holt, "You see how this is going to be?"

"All right." Holt moved toward Doare. "Look here."

Holt gestured toward the upper bunk. Doare gazed up, and Holt kicked him as hard as he could in the right shin.

It hurt Holt's toes but it did the job. Doare grabbed at his leg, and while he was on one knee, Holt hit him in the face.

While Doare flopped backward, Holt turned to block a
punch from Morano, who'd been lounging at the open cell
door all along. The Mexican got in two breath-robbing
shots to the gut, though, before guards arrived to reluctantly
break up the fight.

Which finished things for the short haul, but did nothing
to deter fate. Maybe, Holt thought in the yard as Doare and
Morano stopped in front of him, Lady Chance had written
him for this part all along. She sure hadn't been so sweet
to him these last couple years.

Doare was standing too close, his chest six inches from
Holt's. Holt wanted to wipe his eyes again, but his hand
was busy reaching down into the pocket of his khaki trousers. "Listen," he said.

Morano, to his left and nearly as close as Doare, grinned
and said, "Si?" His teeth were black with rot and his breath
smelled like three-day dead gopher.

"I didn't mean for you to hit your head on that bunk,"
Holt said to Doare. Doare had been knocked cold, and it
was a hell of a job dragging him out of the cell onto the
tier. "Things happen," Holt said to Doare in the yard.

Someone behind Holt laughed.

Holt's pocket inside his pants was slit in half and the two
strips of cloth were tied around a one-by-three slat pried
from the pallet in his cell. Holt worked the club loose from
the knot with his fingers.

"What you figure is going to happen now?" Doare said
to him.

Doare moved just his eyes, and Holt looked down. In
Doare's hand was a length of sharpened metal, a piece of
bedspring—Holt thought incongruously, Doare's got a bed
with springs?—poised an inch from his own abdomen.

Holt took a quick step back, which gave him time to pull
the slat from his britches. Doare was surprised at the movement and made the mistake of lunging. Holt stepped aside
and slammed the slat down at the back of Doare's head,
missed and caught him across the neck instead. The board

snapped in two but Doare went down into the dirt face first anyway. Holt kicked at his temple, and Doare moaned and rolled away.

Morano charged. The guards held the shotguns ready, but did not look otherwise inclined to intercede. Instead of swinging on Holt, Morano ran into him, dropping a shoulder.

Holt flew several feet before landing on his butt. An instant later Morano's bulk was crushing down on him and the Mexican's hands were grabbing for his eyes.

Holt thwacked the short end of the board against Morano's back, to no particular effect. Men circled above them; Holt heard their excited muttering, smelled Morano's fetid breath, saw the thumbs grappling to pop his eyeballs from their sockets—and then Billy Card on Morano's shoulders, tiny as a jockey on a seventeen-hand horse.

Holt balled his fists, extended his arms, and used all his leverage to bring them down together on Morano's ears. Morano screamed and his weight went away. Holt got to his feet as Doare was making it to his knees. Billy was sprawled to one side and scrambling away.

Holt kicked Morano in the head and went on kicking until the Mexican stopped moving. It took long enough to allow Doare to tackle him. Holt went down, but Doare was still groggy, and Holt managed to wriggle away.

The sharpened bedspring lay in the dirt, a few inches from Doare's extended fingers. Holt drove his heel down on Doare's splayed hand and snatched up the makeshift blade. He bent over, was considering the pros and cons of slashing Doare's throat, when a wagonload of bricks crashed down on him. He flopped onto the dirt, fell through it and into a black pit, and descended into bottomless night.

"You attacked fellow inmates without provocation," Quentin Reynolds said.

Holt was morally certain he could not stand erect for more than another few minutes. His ankles were shackled with what had to be ten pounds of iron, his wrists behind his butt with an equal weight of chain. "I'd have to be crazy to pick a fight with Doare and Morano."

Quentin Reynolds did his best not to hear. "You men must learn that your time here will go ever so much more smoothly if you learn to live as civilized beings," Reynolds said smoothly.

The guard at Holt's side was named Kort. Holt remembered catching a glimpse of him a moment before he blacked out. "What'd you hit me with?" Holt asked.

Kort showed Holt a billy club tipped with a leather sack flopping under the weight of lead buckshot.

That explains the double vision, Holt thought.

Quentin Reynolds cleared his throat. He was tall and skeletal as a cow after a bad winter. He wore a starched white shirt with celluloid collar, four-in-hand tie, vest, tailed coat, and striped pants. His voice was flavored with a clipped English tone, his breath with whiskey-stink.

"You could have made something of yourself, sir," Reynolds said.

"You, too, if you'd kept your hands out of the cash box," Holt managed.

Quentin Reynolds's expression darkened. It was common knowledge in the penitentiary that its chief warden, British by birth and American by naturalization, had been chief Indian agent for the western territories, a successful capitalist by the age of forty-two, and a sure shot to go to jail himself for embezzlement at forty-four. But political appointees have connections, and Reynolds's allowed him to trade incarceration for exile here in Yuma.

Quentin Reynolds turned his back to Holt and went to an oak sideboard. Despite the furnishings and absence of bars, the granite walls reminded Holt of his cell. Reynolds poured amber liquor from a crystal decanter, took a sip, sighed, and turned to face Holt once more. "I beg your pardon?" he said politely.

The end result of this interview was foreordained—Holt saw it in the satisfied look on Kort's face—and the hell

with it, Holt thought. "It takes a crook to mind a crook, guv'nor," he said, mocking Reynolds's accent.

Quentin Reynolds emptied his glass. "You, sir . . ."

"The Hole," Holt interrupted.

"Exactly." The warden waved a hand airily at Kort. "Carry on," he said. When he sat down, he slopped his drink and nearly missed his chair.

Kort took Holt's arm. Holt sneered at Reynolds and spat on the carpet; he couldn't see how it could do further harm.

CHAPTER TWO

On the fifth or seventh or ninth day, the hatch opened and Billy Card said, "You're in luck."

"That's me," Holt said. "Luckiest cowpoke in the world."

Billy lowered himself into the dank dimness of the Hole. A dugout with a wooden roof, it was only large enough for him to stretch to his full length and half sit up; a stretch herein was meant to break a man for good and true. The dugout was on the other side of the cell block from the yard, where light could not penetrate, only hellish heat. Once daily the hatch opened and sustenance showered down on Holt—two slices of bread and a bath of iced water that he must lap quickly from the puddles it formed.

Otherwise his company was darkness and silence broken only by the mewling of rats.

Now Billy said, "I'm sorry about this."

"Not your fault." Holt was having trouble seeing in the unaccustomed sunlight streaking through the hatch. "Back to the news: Why am I lucky?"

Billy looked around, as if they might have company. "That Lowell person is back nosing around. I don't think Reynolds wants you to tell about—" Billy turned away again. "—that they got this place," he finished. "Anyway, you're out."

Holt made a vague gesture. "Not yet."

Billy looked distressed. "All you got to do is say everything is hunky-dory."

Holt stared at him. *"Hunky-dory?"*

Billy boosted himself out. "What I mean is everything is jake," he whispered down. "Reynolds said tell you that if you know what you're about, you'll leave out all the parts about Doare and Morano and the warden and the guards, the stuff that'd make him look bad."

Holt followed him into the desert sunshine. "That doesn't leave much to talk about," he said.

It was mid-afternoon, Holt found when he reemerged into the world of the living. A guard walked Holt and Billy up to the third-tier bathing room, where Holt was allowed to wash with coarse soap in a tub of lukewarm water that had been used by other men already. Eyes followed them as they passed back down the balcony, but no one spoke, and Holt saw neither Doare nor Morano. "Doare's still in the infirmary," Billy said in a low voice. "I think you busted his neck bone. And Morano, he won't come at you alone." To the guard he said, pitching his voice a little oddly, "Think it'll rain?"

The guard laughed. "Last time it rained here, I bet Lee was still fighting Grant."

The guard was around twenty. "New on the job?" Holt asked. "How do you like it?"

The guard surprised him. "I'd say there's shenanigans afoot. Me, I'm more the straight and narrow type. Good Christian upbringing, I reckon."

He held open the door and Holt followed Billy inside. "What's your name?"

"Hanratty."

"Pleased to meet you, Mr. Hanratty," Holt said. "Take care of yourself."

The door clanked shut. On his bunk, Holt found a plate with two sandwiches, stringy beef on the coarse white bread that the trustees baked. He hadn't much extra fat on him when he went into the Hole, and now he could feel his ribs. He read the note on the plate as he ate. Over Quentin Reynolds's florid signature, it said he would see Lowell in the morning, and reminded him to mind his p's and q's.

Billy Card was on the top bunk reading a dime novel, scrunched up against the wall so no one could catch him at it. When Holt called Billy on his half-wit act soon after they met, Billy explained that he'd learned early in his life that while folks will pick on a little guy, they generally leave idiots alone, partly from pity, partly from that vague sense of it-could-have-been-me dread that people get from retards.

In fact Billy was smart as a whip, though in a perverse twist of fate his brains got him his ticket to this Arizona penitentiary. After twenty years as a con artist without a single arrest, he swindled the wrong guy, a San Francisco capitalist to whom Billy sold some stock certificates worth only the artistry of Billy's forging skills. This time Billy was nailed. Without any prior convictions, he should have gotten no more than a half year in the county jail; instead, the pissed-off capitalist saw that he ended up looking at four years in Yuma.

Folk also tend to consider dummies harmless, and dummy or not, Billy was that, which is why he'd been made trustee within weeks after his arrival. This allowed him some freedom of movement within the prison's confines, and since people were indiscreet in his presence, Billy was a well of information. In the cell, Holt picked a shred of beef from between his back teeth and said, "What else do you hear about Doare and Morano?"

Billy marked his place in the book with a finger. "You're gonna be okay, least for a while."

"That's nice to know," Holt said.

Later he'd remember the remark, and wonder how he could have been such a sap.

The sandwiches made him feel a bit more human, but he still had plenty enough room for supper a few hours later in the mess hall. The meal was noodles with some kind of dark pork sauce; one of the trustee cooks was a Chinaman, jailed for spitting at a white man.

Lockdown came at seven-thirty. The guard who unlocked

their cell arrived at 7:35, and Morano and three of his thugs stomped in at 7:36.

The last one in closed the barred door behind him, just far enough so the latch didn't click. The three were of a type: big, thick-skulled, and slack-jawed. They closed ranks behind Morano, to block anyone on the tier from seeing what was happening.

Morano pulled a short-barreled .32-caliber Colt's revolver from his pants pocket. "Here's how it is, amigo," he said.

Billy stashed his book under the mattress. "Geez, can I get me one of those?" he said in his dummy voice.

One of the thugs laughed. Morano kept his dark eyes on Holt. "First, you don't make any loud noises, if you don't wish to be *muerte* right now."

"Instead of later?" Holt said, working to keep the fear from his tone. He'd been shot before and did not much like it.

"Oh, you are going to die," Morano said, almost pleasantly. "A gun like this makes little noise, especially if I press it close against your stomach."

Two of the thugs came past Morano, and Holt's arms were pinned behind him. "Because of what happened in the yard?" Holt said incredulously. "That was a fair fight."

"There is no such thing." Morano cocked the revolver and jabbed the muzzle in Holt's gut.

A weapon fired and Holt jerked in instinctive panic, but the report hadn't come from Morano's pistol. It was too deep and loud, and plaster flaked down into Holt's hair. In their surprise, the two men loosened their grip and Holt twisted away, got his hand over Morano's Colt and grappled for the cocked hammer. He missed. Morano pulled the trigger and the hammer came down on Holt's thumb.

Behind Morano the new guard named Hanratty said, "You don't hug the floor this instant, I put the next load in your backs."

Holt jerked the gun away from Morano and raised it quickly over his head, holding it by the barrel. Hanratty nodded, and Holt set it gingerly on the bunk, then scuttled back as Morano and the other three set themselves down, squeezing together like sardines in a can in the tiny floor space. Two more guards charged, their shotguns up. One said to Hanratty, "What the hell are you doing?"

"My job," Hanratty snapped.

Holt moved back into the corner. He felt numb with relief, except for his thumb. It hurt like hell.

Chapter Three

"I might be in danger," Samantha Lowell said.

"I'd help," Holt said dryly, "but . . ." He made a gesture that took in the stone walls of the small room in which they sat facing each other across a wooden table, bare except for Sam's notebook. The shotgun guard standing by the barred door snickered. "Present circumstances and all," Holt finished.

Sam leaned forward. "This business in Utah. I found a witness, a man named Solomon Stein. He described a . . . a being, seven feet tall, features almost like an ape. . . ."

The guard moved to the table and said, "You wanna keep your voice up?"

Sam gave him a pleasant look. "What I'd like, I believe, is to see Warden Reynolds."

"I'm not sure I give a rat's ass what you'd like," the guard said. "What *I'd* like—"

"Is not to see your name in my magazine," Sam interrupted. "How much would you say you make, above your salary, from Doare and Morano's pruno operation alone?"

"Aw Jesus," Holt said, slumping in his chair. He hadn't said anything about it, but the guard would report to Reynolds, and the warden would assume he had.

The guard opened the door and said to someone, "Get the warden." Holt produced his pouch and creased a paper preliminary to building a smoke, studying Sam from the corner of his eye.

Samantha Lowell was as attractive a woman as he'd ever met. She was somewhere in her late twenties, perhaps ten years Holt's junior, with a trim, compact figure, full lips, and high, slightly freckled cheekbones framed by a great cascade of ash-blond hair. She wore a high-necked cotton dress which would have been demure except that against the heat, she'd undone the top button and rolled up the sleeves.

Their first interview a few months earlier had been brief. Flanked by two guards, Sam was working the yard, passing a few words with one man, then another. Something about Holt's answers to her few questions—his name, his crime, his sentence—must have triggered her reporter's instinct, because when she returned, she asked to see him again.

Her beauty discomfited him, and in defense, Holt had been brusque. "What do you want?"

"I read the transcript of your trial," Sam said levelly. "I think you're innocent."

"I am."

"I'm looking for the Big Man," Sam said. "You took the fall for him, didn't you?"

Because it wasn't a question, Holt relaxed a bit. "I'm not sure how much I want to talk about that," he said, "but it's a start."

On her third visit, in this same room, he asked how she'd convinced Reynolds to allow her to see him. "I'm a reporter," she said, "and I'm damned good at what I do." She looked to be sizing him up.

Holt felt edgy once more in the presence of the first woman he'd seen in some time.

"I'll tell you a story," Sam said.

Her background could not have been more different from Holt's if he had grown up Sioux. The first Lowells in the New World were minor British royalty who arrived in 1670, a few years after the English took New York from the Dutch, to assume a huge tract of land on the Hudson granted by the Crown. Fur trading, farming, mercantilism, and shipping interests had left the present generation wealthy and influential. One first cousin owned a fleet of a dozen clippers plying every ocean in the world, she told Holt. Another chaired the largest stock brokerage in New York, while her stepbrother was a member of Congress from the Commonwealth of Massachusetts.

Her father objected, on the basis of unseemliness, when Sam evinced a desire to enter Columbia University to study journalism, but bowed in the face of her will. He even used his influence to help secure her first position.

Harper's Illustrated Weekly was one of the most widely circulated publications in the country, but her first assignment, despite her credentials, was as secretary to the editor. She wrote stories anyway, and their quality soon brought her a promotion to reporter, assigned to cover charity events on Boston's Beacon Hill.

But Sam knew she was destined for greater responsibility, and her determination made it come true. When she first approached Holt, she was the first female correspondent assigned to the frontier in *Harper's* history.

She didn't tell Holt the details of how she'd talked her way into the territorial prison, but he figured that she had politely blackmailed the always vulnerable Quentin Reynolds.

Now the warden himself entered the small room. "Miss Lowell," Reynolds said formally, but did not offer his hand.

"I wonder if I could have perhaps twenty minutes of privacy with Mr. Holt." Sam spread her arms. "As you can see, I haven't brought any cakes with hacksaws baked inside."

"I don't—" Reynolds began.

"Warden," Sam interrupted. "I've already given my word that not only will I—how shall I say it—exercise a certain discretion in my article, but that your portrait within it will be quite flattering. Of course, that promise is contingent on your reasonable cooperation."

Sam stood. "You may search me, if you feel it necessary."

Reynolds blushed. "Twenty minutes," he said. He jerked his head at the guard, turned on his heel and went out, the guard following. When the door clanked shut, Holt turned to see if the guard was eyeing them. He was.

Holt laughed. "You handled that old fraud neatly."

"I'm a pistol, all right," Sam said. "What about Stein's description?"

"It sounds like the Big Man, all right." Holt kept his voice low. "Not that it's going to do me much good."

"Why not?"

Holt counted off the points on his fingers. "First, someone's got to catch him. Second, he's got to talk, and why would he? Third, you'd have to know the right questions to ask—and even I don't have the whole story."

"Who does?"

"The Big Man himself," Holt said, "and whoever hired him."

Sam studied him for a long moment, then sighed. "There's something I didn't tell you," she said. "I wanted to surprise you with good news."

Holt studied her.

"After I decided to believe you," Sam continued, "I wired the magazine's correspondent in Denver and asked him to go up to Argentville and see what he could dig up, beyond the official story, on that woman's murder."

"Cat Lacey." Holt was a touch rankled at her reference to "that woman." He'd had plenty of time to think about Cat, who'd supposedly died at his hand. It might have been the loneliness, but Holt didn't think so; he was pretty sure he'd loved Cat back then.

"A few days after my Denver colleague began nosing around," Sam said, "two men pulled him out of a saloon and into a back alley, and told him to be out of Argentville before morning."

A vague sense of ill ease began to tickle at the back of Holt's mind.

Sam sighed. "Journalists tend to consider themselves invulnerable. Maybe it's because they're always on the outside of the story, describing it but never a part of it. In any case, my colleague decided to stay."

"Aw hell," Holt said. "They killed him."

"Uh-uh," Sam contradicted. "But they made sure he wouldn't ask any more questions. They broke his jaw with an axe handle."

Holt made her a cigarette, struck a match under the lip of the table and lit it for her. She blew out smoke. "But he could still write."

"Meaning?"

"Meaning they told him they'd break something else if he didn't tell them why he was nosing around. He gave them my name."

"You'll be okay if you lay off the Big Man," Holt said, not looking at her.

"Where does that leave you?"

"No better nor worse off than I am now." Holt lit a cigarette of his own. "Actually, that's not entirely true."

Sam pointed to his thumb, the one that had taken the blow from the hammer of Morano's pistol. Overnight it had turned a lovely shade of purple-blue, and it was a toss-up whether he'd lose the fingernail. "What happened?" Sam asked.

"That's what I'm about to tell you," Holt said.

The previous evening, a half hour after the Mexican had come within a heartbeat of punching Holt's ticket, the young guard Hanratty arrived again to let Billy Card out of the cell. Billy was scheduled to swab down the tiers. He enjoyed the job, since it gave him a chance to pick up various pieces of prison scuttlebutt.

To Hanratty, Holt said, "Thanks."

"My dad married late," Hanratty said. "He was near fifty when I was born, and he's seventy-one now. He's got a spread up north of here on the Colorado, but that don't mean much waterwise."

"Longhorns?" Holt said.

Hanratty nodded. "Hundred and fifty head of the stringiest beeves you'd ever want to break a tooth on, and a struggle to raise them. You know what the land's like?"

"Kind where you need cows with mouths ten yards wide moving ten miles an hour to keep fed, like they say."

Hanratty looked surprised. "You've ranched?"

"Like you. When I was a kid."

"Well, I guess I'll be going back to it." Hanratty didn't seem too put out at the notion. "I don't think I'm cut out for this line of work." Hanratty considered. "You can't buck fate."

He was right about his aptitude, Holt decided, when he shut the door gently; most guards liked to slam it, to sound the resolute clang of metal on metal and remind you how shut in you were.

He was right about fate as well, as Holt learned a few hours later when Billy returned from his swamping duties.

"The fight in the yard, and then Morano coming to the cell," Holt said to Sam in the granite-walled room, "that didn't have anything to do with Billy and his dirty pictures, although it was a convenient coincidence that let Doare and Morano obscure what they were really up to. The gun should have tipped me off."

"How so?" Sam crushed her cigarette under her boot heel.

"Doare and Morano operate with Reynolds's coopera-tion," Holt said. "In return, Reynolds gets a cut of the prof-its, and the benefit of Doare and Morano keeping the rest of the men from acting up. But even Reynolds isn't normally going to give Morano a gun—yet that's the only way Morano could have gotten it."

"Which means someone put Reynolds under a lot of pressure, or promised a big payoff," Sam guessed, back in the visitors' room.

"Whoever framed me. Whoever wants you and your Denver friend to keep their noses out of their business." Holt picked a fleck of tobacco from his lip. "Whoever wants me dead."

It hadn't taken much snooping on Billy Card's part to learn the truth; Morano had told him flat out. "Your *compadre*," Morano said as Billy studiously mopped the tier in front of Morano's cell. "He is the walking dead. Today, tomorrow, next week."

Across the table Sam's face had turned pale. She swallowed and made her expression resolute. "That's as good a reason as I can think of not to give it up."

Holt didn't get it.

"I'm going to Utah to find the Big Man," she said. "I'll worry about getting him to talk when the time comes."

"I may not be here by then." Holt waved a hand airily, but truth to tell, he felt far from gay. "Morano is being paid to kill me, and Reynolds is backing him. Sooner or later, my luck will run its string."

The guard entered and said, "Time's up."

Sam snapped, "Go chase yourself," and to Holt's surprise, the guard retreated a few steps, though he remained in the open doorway.

"My people were Lutheran," Holt said. "Pious as a week of Sundays, so I'm toying with the idea of praying." He shook his head. "Problem is, it never did them much good."

"I've got a better idea." Sam was leaning close across the table, so her face was six inches from Holt's. Through the vee between the lapels of her blouse, he could see the swell of the tops of her breasts.

"I'd love to hear it."

"I told you I'm going to Utah." Sam's grin was slightly manic. "Care to come along?" she whispered.

CHAPTER
FOUR

"Why one shoe?" Holt asked.

Billy Card grinned as if he really was the idiot he pretended to be. "I ever tell you I went to college?"

"No." Holt felt hot, edgy, and possessed with the mental image of a load of buckshot shredding into his back.

"You notice it's not laced up," Billy said proudly, as if he'd just discovered a cure for the cold.

Holt tried to put a rein on his antsiness. "Billy," he said. "What the goddamn hell are you talking about?"

"Colorado State Normal School," Billy said. "I was gonna be a teacher."

"Good for you."

"That college," Billy said. "They had a running team. I won a gold medal, fourteen-carat."

"You still got it?" Holt felt as if the conversation, and this day, had descended into the surreal.

"Hell no," Billy said. "I pawned it the day after I won it. Got twenty bucks." He waved his shod foot, the right; his left was bare. "It's not laced, so I can get rid of it quick," Billy said, "and also so there's room for the rock."

"Mind that you don't break your toes."

"I've done this before," Billy said.

Holt gazed across the yard. All seemed normal, and Holt saw no suspicion on the faces of the guards lounging in the veranda's shade. Doare was still in the infirmary, and Morano, though prone to giving Holt dark glances, had not confronted him again. "You sure you don't want to come along?" Holt said to Billy.

"I got a lot of good-behavior time built up," Billy said. "Six months more and I'm on my way. I guess I'll stick it out."

Holt studied the guards. "Tell me again."

"Jeez, are you getting goofy from the sun?" Billy was enjoying himself. He pointed to a section of the wall to their backs. "Stand just to the side," he said. "Be a shame if you went before you went, so to speak."

"How'd she tell you?" Holt asked.

"She was here this morning."

"She didn't want to see me?" Holt felt embarrassed as soon as the words were out.

"You think that would have been a good idea?" Billy teased. He dry-washed his hand and studied the sun, which was near directly overhead. "Time for business."

Billy offered his hand. Holt shook it. Billy said, "Good luck, pard. See you in church."

Morano frowned curiously as Billy strode in his direction. Holt heard Morano say, "What you want, *niño*?"

Holt backed toward the section of the high wall that Billy had indicated. He felt the stone touch his back.

Across the yard, Billy reached Morano and said, *"Hola, amigo. Que pasa pasa pasa?"*

Morano smiled uncertainly, and Billy stomped down on his foot with the shoe containing the rock.

Morano let out an unholy scream. Billy kicked off the shoe and took off. Morano stumbled after him, gimpily at first and then in earnest, his anger overtaking his pain. Other prisoners formed a train behind Morano, and now the guards were on their feet, cons and warders both amused at any break from the somnolent routine.

As Billy darted for the far corner of the yard with most of the present company in pursuit, the wall beside Holt exploded in a great blast of rock and dust. Holt flattened himself beside the hole that appeared, although a chunk of granite grazed across his cheek, peeling skin from flesh.

Holt plunged into the roiling cloud of debris, holding his breath and closing his nostrils. The shotgun blast he'd envisioned did not come until he emerged, and then only faintly, though he heard the pellets plinking into the wall behind him as he reached daylight. A moment later the weight of the rock above the hole in the wall collapsed and a couple dozen tons of granite closed into the space through which he'd come.

Samantha Lowell sat a roan mare and held the bridle reins to another horse, a bay gelding that was on the edge of bolting in reaction to the explosion. Holt vaulted into the saddle and dug the heels of his prison shoes into its flanks, jerking the reins from Sam's hand to pull the horse's head up. The horse pranced back three steps and prepared to rear. Holt slapped it across the top of the head.

A sere wind blew away the last of the dust, and Holt realized he and Sam were not alone. The oldest man Holt had ever seen was horseback beyond Sam, his hands folded across the saddle horn. "You know how to handle a animal," he observed. He wore denim coveralls over a red union suit. Long wattles hung down beneath his chin, and he was bald as an eagle except for two swatches of snowy hair that stood up on either side of his pate.

The old man cantered his horse over next to Holt and offered his hand. "Henry P. Terwilliger," he said. "Powderman, by profession."

Holt glanced back at the collapsed wall. "I hope to shout," he said.

From the opening came the noise of another diffuse shotgun round, and guards' and prisoners' excited voices. Someone clambered over the debris, a shotgun fired, and the figure threw up both arms and fell facedown. For one desperate moment Holt thought it was Billy Card, but then, in the final throe of death, the man flopped onto his back and Holt saw it was only some stranger trying to take advantage of the moment.

Henry P. Terwilliger noted the blood oozing from the two dozen exit wounds in the man's chest. "Guess it's time to mosey," he said. He spurred his horse and Sam did the same.

Holt brought up the rear, keeping close behind Sam. Sure enough, a half mile down the gravel road that approached the prison, her roan pulled up short and made a perfunctory effort to throw her. Holt grabbed the bridle rein in a manner that told the horse to cut the nonsense. The roan nicked and lowered its head.

Sam did not look frightened; the flush on her face seemed to reflect excitement. The roan was calmed now, and Sam reached across and put her hand over Holt's. She had not touched him previously, and he could feel the warmth of her flesh. Truth to tell he liked it, and she might have sensed that before she pulled back.

"Bunch of muggins," Henry P. Terwilliger said.

"How's that?" Holt asked.

"Them guards," Terwilliger said. "Jeez, I ain't had so much fun since a wagon run down my dogs."

Sam mopped up some gravy with a piece of bread. "I feel claustrophobic."

"What's that mean?" Terwilliger said, sounding insulted.

The only light came from a kerosene lantern sitting in their midst. Occasionally the wick flared to throw grotesque shadows on the walls and ceiling of the mine that Terwilliger, Holt had learned, spent a good part of the last decade prospecting. By Holt's count they were two hundred paces into its depths; the horses were picketed within the mouth, where a spring rivulet seeped from the wall.

"What's this?" Holt showed Terwilliger a piece of meat that he'd speared on the tip of the knife Sam had given him.

"Rat," Terwilliger said. "Nice fat desert rat."

Sam gulped. "It tastes like chicken."

"Everything does," Terwilliger said. He chowed down on another piece of meat. "You innocent?" he asked Holt.

"Yeah."

"That's what they all say." Terwilliger was interested in other things. "Ask me how I done it."

"How'd you do it?" Holt said.

"At night. The missy here"—Terwilliger indicated Sam

with his knife—"she offers me five hundred gold to blow that wall."

"Where'd you find him?" Holt asked Sam.

"Everyone knows Henry P. Terwilliger," the old prospector put in. "You think I ever took five hundred out of this hole?"

At least he'd tried, Holt could see. The shaft, burrowing into the side of a mesa, was nicely timbered, with clean vertical walls whose quartz sparkled in the lamplight. In the dead end where they sat, bore holes awaited charges. "Did you?" Holt asked.

"Hell no," Terwilliger said. "But I'm one corker of a blaster."

"They don't pay much attention to the walls at night," Sam said. She set aside her plate, looking a little green.

"The mortar is softer 'n the rock," Terwilliger said with an expert's pride. "You can drill it with a hand auger, which is what I did. A few charges of giant powder, twine the fuses together, and prime 'em. When you come back later, all's you got to do is strike a match, and Bob's your uncle."

"Bob's your uncle?" Holt echoed.

"British expression," Sam said. "It means everything is fine."

"My mother on my father's side," Terwilliger said, sounding much like Billy Card doing his act. "Born in Sussex."

"Is that a fact?" Holt said, entertaining thoughts about the fat and the frying pan. Holt got out his pouch and went to work on a cigarette, mostly so he wouldn't have to look at Sam. "What now?"

"Well, let me see." The irony in her tone was evident. "You're a fugitive from justice, and I'm a pretty sure bet as an accessory. I'd say we're both in deep trouble, unless we head up to Utah, find the Big Man, and somehow force him to exonerate you."

"That seems simple enough," Holt said. "I feel a lot better now that we've worked that out."

Henry P. Terwilliger pointed his knife at Sam's plate, still half full of stew. "Are you gonna finish that rat?" he inquired politely.

CHAPTER FIVE

The climate turned less brutal after Holt and Sam took their leave of Henry P. Terwilliger and rode north. By the time they reached the high country of the upstream Colorado, the days were bright with no more than a feather of clouds, and the star-spackled nights were pleasantly chill, even in mid-August.

They crossed the river on the suspension bridge spanning Marble Canyon. Rapids crashed past rocks two hundred feet below the bridge's slats, and Holt had to blindfold the horses and walk them across one at a time, while Sam waited on the far side.

Holt wouldn't have minded a blindfold himself. As a boy, he'd fallen from the roof of his father's barn while mending shingles, and though he'd landed unhurt in hay-strewn mud, he'd disliked heights ever since. But his vanity was stronger than his fear on this occasion, so as he marched the horses across, he gazed at Sam with a strained smile as if he were being nonchalant instead of avoiding the neurotic urge to look down.

In the ten days they'd been on the trail, Holt had been working to grow comfortable with her, and although she made it easy enough, he was still only about three-quarters of the way there. Evenings were roughest, that time after they'd eaten and he'd thrown another chunk of scrub oak on the fire and built them both smokes, and felt there was something he should bring up but couldn't quite figure what it was.

"You sit the saddle pretty handy," Holt said now as they put the river to their backs. "Where'd you learn?"

"Central Park." When he shook his head, she explained, "In New York City, when I was in college. There's a riding stable there."

"I never been more than a hundred miles east of the Mississippi," Holt said, "and that was back when I was a kid. I'm not counting the war."

Her attention perked up. She'd asked a few innocuous questions in the course of their journey, but Holt, for reasons obscure to him, did not encourage her inquiries, and she had not pushed them.

Late that afternoon they came on a Kanab Indian village. Naked children came racing out to meet them, jabbering excitedly and plucking at the cuffs of Sam's britches, so Holt followed the kids into the camp. He shook hands with the headman, spoke to him in Spanish, and made him a gift of a half pound of coffee and a pouch of tobacco. The headman was a handsome fellow about Holt's age, and after he thanked Holt, he went to Sam, sitting her roan and stroking the animal's forehead. *"Usted eres una mujer muy linda,"* he said.

Sam smiled. "Thank you."

The headman cocked his chin in Holt's direction. *"El tiene mas suerte."*

Holt blushed and thought, that's me all right; lucky in love.

They camped another half-dozen miles on, among cottonwoods lining the bank of a creek tributary of the Colorado. Holt reckoned they were within shouting distance of the Utah line. He picketed the horses and undid the rucksacks, while Sam gathered dead wood from along the high-water line of the creek, and fallen leaves for tinder. "I figure on paying you back," Holt said.

Sam blew on the smoldering leaves. "How's that?"

"For rigging us out." Holt wrestled the saddle from the roan. The horses, tack, cook gear, provisions, and clothing she'd obtained before the breakout must have cost her several hundred, and two days out of Yuma she'd gone alone into a town named Buckeye and come back with a Winchester lever-action long gun and two Colt's revolvers, a .45 for him and a .38 for herself, with holsters and several boxes of cartridges.

When she returned from Buckeye, Sam had a sly look. After she dismounted, she presented him with a small hinged box. Inside, resting on velvet, was a Hamilton watch on a gold-plated chain. Holt was touched; he'd never owned a watch before.

Holt set his saddle near the fire ring for a back rest. "I should maybe show you a few things about using it."

Sam gave him an exasperated look. "Anyone ever point out you have a tendency to talk in shorthand?"

"The handgun."

"You figure I might want to shoot someone?"

"No one wants to." Holt got out the coffeepot. "But that's what it's for."

Sam studied the fire.

"You can hunt with a long gun," Holt said, "but a revolver is only good for shooting snakes and men." Holt considered. "Which is sometimes the same thing."

He took the pot and rifle down to the water and went upstream a couple hundred yards, moving silently, but no deer flushed from the brush. Instead they had beans with bacon, coffee, and two roasted ears of corn that the Kanab headman had given Holt. After they'd smoked, Holt checked the loads in Sam's .38, scooped up the empty tin that had held the beans, and led Sam down to the creek.

He hung the tin on a branch and backed up twenty paces. "Any further and your chances of hitting what you're aiming at, best of circumstances, gets to be a matter of luck."

Holt handed her the revolver. It was a double action, so he had her fire off a round just pulling the trigger, to let her see that the resistance was substantial, then had her cock the hammer first. On the last shot of the cylinder, she nicked the tin's bottom. Holt reloaded for her. Around the third shot, he found himself close behind, his arms reaching around to help her steady the gun. "I like this," Sam said in a soft voice.

"What?" Holt fairly yelped. He released her and shied away.

"Learning to shoot," Sam said levelly, but he could tell by her eyes that she was teasing him a little.

When twilight ended the lesson, Holt put the pot on to reheat what was left of the coffee. As he poured a half cup for each of them, Sam said, "Let's chat."

The coffee had turned thick and strong, the way Holt liked it. "About what?"

"I don't know," Sam said airily. "Tell me a tale."

In Yuma he'd worked hard at forgetting the past and living for the day, and now, as he set another chuck of summer-dried driftwood on the fire, he had trouble getting started. Sam listened without interrupting except for an encouraging murmur now and then, and presently he found himself talking about bygone days, at first wondering why he was telling her these things about who he had been, but after a while comfortable with it all, the story and the fire's warmth and a good smoke and her company.

The time east of the Mississippi he'd mentioned earlier that day, ended when he was five years old, because his father, though hardworking, was innately peripatetic. From a homestead in Illinois, he moved the family to Kansas, and a few years after that to southern Idaho, where he took up road ranching along the Oregon Trail. In the summer, the pilgrims arrived with depleted oxen; Holt's father traded them fresh stock, one fat healthy animal for two rib-racked yoke oxen. In the winter, the family moved two hundred miles north to the clement confines of the Beaverhead valley in Montana, where the animals fed on dried range grass and grew meaty once again. Finally, when Holt was twelve and his father had saved up a grubstake, they settled for good in the broad Bitterroot valley, taking up on a section close by the meandering river.

His father had left the Rhine and his schooling when he

was four, traveling steerage to the New World; Holt's mother, in contrast, was from Connecticut stock that had been in the U.S. for three generations. She graduated from Blessed Sacrament College for Women in New Haven, and meant to take up schoolteaching until she fell in love with Matthew Holt and the adventure of frontiering.

Because they moved so often, Holt's education was limited to his mother's tutelage in reading, writing, and ciphering. From his father he gained a restlessness and sufficient introduction to hard work to show him he was not cut out to be an agriculturist. In the winter of 1863, two weeks after Lincoln's Emancipation Proclamation, Holt enlisted in the Union Army.

In memory his term as a bluecoat was a two-year blur of marching, mud, cold food or none, and tedium broken by terror. It ended abruptly on a sweltering April day near Vicksburg, Mississippi. Holt was walking down a lane within sight of the river toward a farm where, rumor had it, a man could get a cool drink of buttermilk, when some gray-clad he never knew nor saw shot him in the back.

"I was lucky," Holt said to Sam as they lounged by the fire.

"To get shot?"

"To get fixed. You ever hear of Harvard?"

"The college?" She was teasing him again. "I believe I have."

"That's where this doctor went to school."

"Which doctor?"

"The one who took the minié ball out of me."

The bullet had nicked his spine; a half inch to the right and he would have been paralyzed or dead, the doctor told him. Instead he mended, with no aftereffect beyond a tendency to get a little achy after a long day in the saddle.

"Actually, there's one other thing," Holt said to Sam.

"What?"

"It's a little embarrassing." Holt flicked the butt of his cigarette into the fire.

Sam reclined on the grassy creek bed, her head propped on her saddle. To Holt she looked swell.

"It spooked me some."

"Getting shot?" Sam said. "I imagine it would."

"I'm not superstitious," Holt said, "but I was left with this feeling that next time it's going to get me for true."

"Why should there be a next time?"

"We're on the run," Holt said, "and in a day or so, luck willing, I'll be facing one mean big son of a bitch."

Sam shifted languidly to her side. "Oh yeah," she said. "I almost forgot."

After healing, Holt returned to Montana, to find that his father had died in a horse fall a month earlier. They buried him beside the house in the shadow of the snow-glazed Bitterroot mountains.

If Holt had little stomach for taking over the ranch before he'd enlisted, he was plumb uninterested now. He hung around long enough to help his mother sell the spread and to drive her by wagon to the gold camp at Virginia City. There he put her on a stage for the beginning of a long journey that would end in New Haven, where she planned to take up teaching after all.

"I got into the law enforcement profession," Holt said to Sam. "I worked here and there around the West, town marshal, deputy sheriff, that sort of thing. Like my daddy, I had trouble staying put, but that was okay. I got to scratch the itch and make some honest dollars. But then I hit Argentville."

The roan nickered and Sam stretched, her breasts straining against the cotton of her blouse. "I wish you wouldn't do that," Holt blurted out, and immediately wanted to swallow his words.

"Do what?" she said.

"Never mind," Holt said, too sharply. "Argentville," he repeated.

"Where this story really starts," Sam guessed.

Holt stared at the fire. "Right. There's some more embarrassing stuff, though."

Sam laughed, and Holt tried not to mind her teasing. "I guess I can stand it," she said.

Cat Lacey, Holt decided as he went on with his story, was not Sam's equal in beauty, although he did not mention that part to Sam. Cat had been some places and done some things, and the years had not been completely kind. When Holt met her in the high-mountain Colorado silver camp that some classicist dubbed Argentville, she was running the settlement's principal house of pleasure, though she had retired from personally entertaining any customers.

She and Holt hit it off from the start. Although he was town marshal and she a madam, within two weeks of his arrival they were tight as ticks. Stranger things had happened in the course of Holt's various careers, and no one made an issue of the relationship—at least not at first.

"I wanted to get that part of the story out of the way right off," Holt said to Sam by the fire.

"That's the embarrassing part?" Sam scoffed. "That you were lovers with a former prostitute? Tsk tsk."

Holt ignored her sarcasm and plunged ahead. The reason it was okay for a lawman to take up with a whore was because prostitution was legal in Argentville, even if the codes of the state of Colorado begged to differ. It helped keep the workers happy, which made the Company happy. Argentville *was* the Company, and one way or another, nearly every man toiled for its profit.

The Argentville boom began a few summers before Holt's arrival, when a modestly successful shopkeeper named Maynard Fitzsimmons grubstaked two Lithuanian bummers for twenty-three dollars and a jug of moonshine. In those days the town was a nameless tent city with a population of maybe three dozen gold seekers.

So it was free gold the Lithuanians were looking for when they climbed Argent Hill, where they drained the jug and promptly passed out. The next morning, in a fit of hungover remorse, they went to work, digging straight down on the spot where they'd napped, thinking to stockpile gravel for eventual washing.

At nine feet they hit a vein—not of gold, but the richest carbonate silver ore that God ever set on this planet. A month later Fitzsimmons used the profits of his share to buy out the Lithuanians for a hundred thousand each; by the end of that year Fitzsimmons was a millionaire. Other strikes were made over time, but Fitzsimmons had the head start, and the wherewithal to acquire them before they proved out. Some didn't, but many did, and by and by Fitzsimmons pretty much owned the mountain. That sealed Argentville's future. Silver mining was not like panning for gold; it was labor-intensive, and required a labor force, plentiful dynamite, heavy machinery, and a nearby smelter.

When Holt rode in, he found a full-fledged town, with a bank, newspaper, and two-story opera house with Doric columns. It also boasted four saloons, a casino, two whorehouses in addition to the one run by Cat Lacey, and a Miners' Union, all controlled by one Jack Stringer.

Stringer had drifted into town within weeks of Fitzsimmons's lucky strike, toting six thousand dollars and a cloudy reputation. Holt did not know how Stringer had arranged an accommodation with Fitzsimmons, but he could guess.

"Given that plentiful vice was good for labor relations," Holt told Sam, "Fitzsimmons figured if it was in the open, there was less chance for trouble. But Fitzsimmons didn't need the money or the additional headache, and he could see Stringer made a better ally than an enemy, so essentially he let Stringer have the franchise."

"Where did the Miners' Union fit in with Stringer's interests?" Sam asked.

"Mostly, it fit in with Fitzsimmons's. Stringer worked in cahoots with him. They'd draw up a niggardly contract, and then Stringer would put the word out to the workers that if the deal wasn't ratified, bones would be broken."

"So he was a thug."

Holt shook his head no. "That's the funny thing. Stringer had thugs working for him, but he's smooth as lamp oil himself. Good-looking, soft-spoken, nice dress, obviously had schooling—I almost liked him. Hell, I *did* like him. We got drunk together a few times."

Holt watched Sam make her mouth into an O and blow a smoke ring. "Fitzsimmons—the so-called legitimate businessman—was the one who galled an hombre," Holt went on. "All that cash money had gone to his head. He was mean-spirited and mean-pursed, greedy as all get-out, and he had about a two-inch fuse on his temper, especially when he didn't get his way."

"He was the one who hired you?"

"Yeah, and I figured I could live with him being the way he was. I was trying to be philosophical, tell myself that a bad personality didn't mean a man was bad through and through." Holt shrugged. "I was wrong. He was maybe bad enough to murder."

"Anyone in particular?"

"Cat Lacey had her habits," Holt said, not answering the question. "The woman who was my . . . friend . . ."

"I'm paying attention," Sam said. "I remember who Cat Lacey was."

Jeez, Holt thought, but he certainly did have one hell of a knack for giving her opportunities to needle him. "One habit was laudanum. Sometimes it made her nod off, but other times it loosened her tongue. She was pretty doped up the night she told me."

"Told you what?"

"What happened to the boy who was marshal before me," Holt said.

There was no crime in Argentville; Stringer's gang saw to that. Fitzsimmons only replaced Holt's predecessor to mollify a new and vocal segment of the citizenry.

With the increasing civilization of Argentville, women had begun to arrive—not the sort in Cat's stable, but sturdy housewives whose husbands worked down in the mines.

They took exception to some of Stringer's more unsavory pursuits and demanded that Fitzsimmons do something about them. Stringer couldn't very well threaten the women as he did the men, so to forestall their objections, Fitzsimmons hired the first marshal.

His name, Cat told Holt in her opium daze, was Luis Sanchez, and Fitzsimmons picked him because the mining magnate reckoned that a Mexican this far north would be thankful for any job and would toe Fitzsimmons's line. Instead, it turned out that Sanchez was a good Catholic with backbone enough to by-God take the job seriously.

A week after Sanchez was hired, one of Fitzsimmons's foremen beat the living daylights out of a Company blaster who miscalculated a powder charge and blew in a stope. Sanchez arrested the foreman and, accompanied by the blaster's wife, marched the foreman to Fitzsimmons and demanded charges be brought, on pain of bringing the matter to the attention of the state attorney general in Denver.

Fitzsimmons was livid, but his hands were tied. The foreman was tried, convicted, sentenced to the state penitentiary, and "escaped" while being transported. Fitzsimmons then attempted to fire Sanchez, and found himself facing an angry mob of local women. Fitzsimmons backed down, but privately told Sanchez to lay off if he knew what was good for him.

Instead, Sanchez turned in Stringer's direction, launching a reform campaign to shut down Stringer's vice houses. But Sanchez had more *cojones* than prudence: He'd now forced the hand of Stringer, and likely Fitzsimmons.

Two days later Sanchez was shot in the stomach, chest, and temple as he lay naked upstairs in Cat Lacey's place, while his whore was returning down the hall after seeing to her ablutions.

Responding to the noise of the gunfire, and a moment later the girl's screams, Cat reached the second-floor room in time to see two hands hooked over the sill of the open window. They let go, and Cat heard a heavy thud as the murderer hit the ground. Cat got to the window in time to see him pick himself up and rattle hocks down the alley.

Did she recognize him? Holt asked when Cat finished her story. She told him no, nor did she get a look at his face. But she'd know him if she ever saw him again.

If she didn't see his features, how could she identify him?

"Because he was hardly a man," Holt answered his rhetorical question, telling the story to Sam. "He was more like a monster—near seven feet tall, huge and broad and ropy, with a gait like some circus ape and a head way too large even for a body like that."

"The Big Man," Sam said.

Holt nodded. "I'd reckon so," he said.

CHAPTER SIX

They breakfasted on coffee and hardtack spread with home-canned jam they'd bought from a farm wife outside Flagstaff, and were on the trail before Holt's new watch struck eight, riding in companionable silence. An hour on, the rutted wagon tracks they were following suddenly widened and turned into a proper gravel road that must have been graded with a horse-team scraper no longer ago than that spring.

"Welcome to Utah," Holt said. "Nice territory if you don't mind scrub brush and Mormons."

"What about scrub brush and Mormons?"

"Utah's got plenty of both," Holt said.

Despite the many days in the saddle, she looked fresh and cleaner than Holt felt. He wondered if they were far enough from Yuma to chance taking hotel rooms this night; they had to be within ten miles of one of the Mormon settlements. Maybe not *rooms*, but *a* room, Holt thought idly, and immediately chastized himself for a fool.

"Stop teasing me," Sam said.

Holt was startled and began to blush, before realizing that she was referring to his story, not his thoughts. "Oh, you can take it but you can't dish it out," he recovered.

"That's right," Sam said, mock-solemn. "I'll do the teasing around here."

Holt cantered his horse up beside hers. "Fitzsimmons and Stringer had a falling out, and I got caught in the middle."

"I'd imagine you'd take a lesson from Sanchez's fate."

"I did, and I was about to turn my back on the job, but I got hind-footed. All of a sudden, if I walked out, men were going to be hurt bad, in the wallet and otherwise. I thought I could forestall a bad situation."

"Did you?"

"To this day, I don't know," Holt said. "What I do know is the situation sure enough turned bad for me."

Before Holt could make up his mind whether to seek Sanchez's murderer or hit the trail, notices went up in the changing room of every one of Maynard Fitzsimmons's mines, announcing that due to the fall in the market price of silver, everyone would have to make sacrifices.

Fitzsimmons's sacrifice was to cut the miners' day wage from five dollars to three—and, the notice suggested without much subtlety, the union could go chase its tail.

In his usual blustering way, Fitzsimmons made this move without consulting Stringer. This might have been calculated, Fitzsimmons's way of demonstrating his power to Stringer. If so, it didn't work; instead, it brought up the looming specter of a full-out labor war, a possibility that kept Holt in town.

Because Fitzsimmons was pleased with what he perceived as a bold step, he bragged to Holt about his brilliant strategy. One of Stringer's thugs was actually on Fitzsimmons's payroll, so he knew that the gambler could not order a work stoppage—because it would reveal that Stringer had embezzled thousands of dollars from the union strike fund.

But the next day, Stringer called and raised Fitzsimmons's bet by calling a strike after all. According to Fitzsimmons's spy, Stringer had sufficient cash on hand to pay benefits for two weeks; further, Stringer himself came to Fitzsimmons to suggest that if he didn't restore wages, giant powder was going to explode in some extremely inconvenient places.

Within an hour of this interview, Fitzsimmons posted a new set of notices, stating that if the miners did not return to their labors within twenty-four hours, or if sabotage occurred, he'd bring in Pinkertons. The brutality of the detective agency's strikebreakers was legendary. Every man knew that they'd make Stringer's goons look like the Ladies' Knitting Society.

"Talk about goons," Holt said to Sam. "I was the biggest goon of all."

"How so?"

"The whole business had nothing to do with wages or the price of silver or Stringer's strike fund."

Sam thought a moment. "Fitzsimmons and Stringer had decided to fight for control of Argentville, winner take all."

Holt was surprised. "How'd you guess?"

A mule deer bolted from a thicket, startling Sam's horse. She jerked hard on the reins and it behaved. "Reporter's instinct," she answered.

Holt watched the deer lope away from them. "Wish I'd had me some of that," he said glumly.

Yuma gave Holt time to ponder on why he'd lived at all. His best guess was that the murders of two law officers inside three months would bring Argentville more attention than either Fitzsimmons or Stringer needed.

His first step was to ask Fitzsimmons to compromise on a lesser pay cut, or a suspension of the salary reduction, pending negotiation of a new contract with the miners. When that didn't work, he threatened to petition the Colorado governor to send in the state militia to keep the peace. Fitzsimmons stood firm.

Holt went to Stringer and suggested he suspend the strike for the three days it would take Holt to ride round-trip to Denver. Stringer was suave, polite, and turned Holt down absolutely. "Those Pinkertons might do the men a favor," Stringer said. "If push comes to shove, they're not going to take it lying down."

What he meant was that a few killings might bring on the war that could topple his rival Fitzsimmons.

Holt saw no alternative but to head for Denver the next

morning. In the meantime he warned Stringer he'd bring in the state to shut down his bordellos, and warned Fitzsimmons that violence would bring a full investigation into the magnate's responsibility.

"It didn't work," Sam surmised as they rode north.

"Not a bit," Holt said. "So, seeing how well I was handling the situation, I decided to do something really smart. I visited Cat and told her my troubles, while she sipped from those little brown bottles of laudanum, and I drank maybe a half quart of bourbon. When I came around, it was morning."

Holt reined up and Sam turned her horse to face him. "I was sitting on the carpet of Cat's apartment, leaned up against her divan where she reclined. There was a knife in her brisket and my hand was around the haft."

"Oh my," Sam said.

"Also, we weren't alone. This dapper jasper was standing just inside the door, wearing a gold star. He was Clennon Pert, Federal Marshal."

"What was a federal marshal doing in Argentville?"

"One of a long set of good questions without answers," Holt said. "Suffice to say that his immediate purpose was to arrest me for murder. Pert took me down to Denver and put me in a jail cell. After time, two lawyers appeared, the prosecuting attorney and a lawyer for me. I never knew who engaged him or paid his fee."

Holt stared into the middle distance, as if searching for his fate. "They told me that I could have a trial, but if I did, I was going to be hung. Otherwise, they'd agree to send me to Yuma for the rest of my days."

"Some choice," Sam said.

"I'm trying to look on the bright side," Holt said. "For the time being, I'm neither dead nor in Yuma."

The road brought them to the settlement called Kingdom around suppertime. Holt declared it good timing and decided they'd get those rooms and bath he'd been hankering for. Sam didn't object.

Kingdom was a dozen frame houses, café, town hall, mercantile, feed and grain, hotel, and livery. This being Utah, there was no saloon, but after Holt got the horses installed and fed in the livery, he made discreet inquiry, and the hosteler provided him with an unlabeled bottle of brown liquor that wasn't overly hard on the gut. In the hotel bathroom, Holt sipped on it while he lay up to his neck in the soapy water, and by the time he met Sam in the café, he felt mildly merry.

Her appearance enhanced his mood: She had changed into a clean blouse and a leather skirt, and her hair was up in some kind of swirl atop her head. "I bought it in that general store," she said. "The skirt, I mean."

"It suits you," Holt said. He was mildly startled when she lowered her eyes modestly.

They ordered steak and fried potatoes, and the waitress brought coffee without asking, and while they sipped it, Holt said, "You know how you see something midday and all of a sudden it triggers recollection of a dream?"

Sam smiled wryly. "What are you talking about?"

"It happened the day after Pert arrested me, except what I recollected wasn't a dream. I must have come partway out of my drunk while Cat was killed. I saw him."

Half of the café's six tables were occupied, and the patrons gave every sign of being solid, sober burghers. "Cat wasn't exaggerating. His head was big as a bucket and almost touched the ceiling, and he was about as broad as a barn door."

"Did you see his face?"

Holt shook his head no. "But if God made more than one like him, He's got an odd sense of humor."

The waitress brought their plates, and Holt sawed off a piece of steak. It was tender and sweet with juice, and he murmured in satisfaction. "The question is whether he was working for Stringer, Fitzsimmons, or Pert."

"Why would Pert frame you?"

"For money," Holt said.

"I could check on him, find out what sort of reputation he has."

"Not now you can't. We're on our own."

They had hand-churned vanilla ice cream for dessert, and Holt walked Sam to her room, adjacent to his. "We'll want an early start."

"I'll meet you downstairs at six," Sam said. "Sleep well."

Before Holt could craft a response, her door opened and closed and she was gone. When he hit the hay, her nearness agitated him enough to keep sleep away until the early hours of the morning.

CHAPTER
SEVEN

Holt's back where the minié ball had caught him was aching more than somewhat, and he was trying not to act cranky. The town of Kingdom was a day and night behind them, and Holt's brief flirtation with the idea of him and Sam coming closer together seemed to be paying off in continued nocturnal restlessness.

Their course ran roughly northeast, in parallel to the Colorado, though the river was out of sight across twenty miles of desert to their right. The land was mostly flat, interrupted by the occasional butte. In country like this, distance was deceptive, and it seemed to take forever to cover any miles.

Soon after they took their lunch, though, the road rose toward a low pass. "You sure this is the right way?" Holt asked.

"When I visited Golem the other time, I came by stage from Salt Lake City, other direction," she said. "All I know is what that pilgrim told us."

Another butte flanked the crest of the pass up ahead, the road passing within fifty feet of its gullied sidewall. They'd encountered the pilgrim a few hours back. He rode alone and without a pack animal, armed with rifle, handgun, and a look that said he knew how to use both. Sam did the talking, but the man was plenty more interested in Holt.

Now Holt sighed. "How much water you got left?"

Sam rattled the canteen hanging by a leather thong from her saddle horn. "Maybe a handful."

"Swell," Holt muttered. "Just dandy." He bent to check his own canteen.

A rifle went off with a sharp crack, and a bullet whistled a foot above Holt's head.

Holt tumbled from the saddle but kept hold of the reins, jerked the gelding around to put it between himself and the butte from which the shot had come. Sam was right behind him, following the lead of his move. The cover of the horses stopped the bushwhacker for the moment. One of those sorts who'll shoot a man, Holt thought sourly, but hates to waste a good horse.

Ten yards off the track, Holt spotted a thicket of grease-wood flanked by a good-sized boulder. He pointed and Sam nodded. She was afraid all right, but that was good; he'd have worried if she weren't. "You make for the rock," he said in a low voice. "When I say 'now.' "

"What about the horses?"

"They're not going anywhere. Pay attention."

She did.

"Now!"

She was closer to the rock, but he caught up as they reached it just before another shot rang out. Holt grabbed Sam's arm at the elbow and threw her down behind the boulder, then fell atop her.

"What's next?" Her face was close enough to his that he could feel the warmth of her ragged breathing.

"He can keep us pinned long as he wants," Holt thought out loud. "He's likely to have food and water. On the other hand, for the moment it's a Mexican standoff."

"Probably it's safe to get off me now," Sam said.

Holt did, then removed his neckerchief, spread it over his palm, and began to thumb cartridges from the loops on Sam's holster belt. "We got to take the initiative before we're too thirsty to cope." He dropped a fistful of cartridges in the midst of the red square of cotton and had her turn over so he could get to those at her back.

A voice hollered, "Holt."

Holt rose above the corner and fired a shot in that general direction. "That pretty much settles the issue." Holt smiled wryly. "At least we know we're on the road to Golem. He couldn't chance us running into someone else who would tell us we'd gotten a bum steer. He wanted to be sure we'd walk into his ambush."

Behind the cover of the rock, the land sloped away. "Ought to take me less than a half hour." He set down the cartridges so the neckerchief protected them from the gritty dirt. "You fire every couple of minutes or any time he fires at you. Don't worry about aiming."

"I could get lucky," Sam said.

"Just keep your head down," Holt said, "and reload every time you let off a shot." He crab-walked away, keeping the thicket between him and the gunman. When he was sure he was below the man's horizon line, Holt straightened and started to circle around.

By the time he reached the butte's skirt, Holt knew from the rifle reports that the gunman was holed up at the foot of a gully tangent to the line of the road. Holt would have preferred to circle around and come in from behind, but the butte had to be a half mile across. By the time he made it, Sam would be hurting for water; for that matter, so would he.

Sam fired. The gunman laughed and called out Holt's name and a curse word, as he had periodically. Otherwise he was saving his ammunition.

Holt moved along the butte's edge, waited for Sam's next shot, and made his move on its echo, diving into the cover of the gully adjacent to that which hid their attacker. When he got his breath back, he started up the steep ditch, placing his boots carefully and silently in the crumbly marl.

He was twenty feet up when his feet slipped out from under him. He clawed at the rock but managed only to get turned on his back with his feet facing downhill before he was sliding down the chute like a sledge on hard-packed snow.

When he hit bottom and sat up, the gunman stood a few

yards away, his Colt leveled down at Holt's chest. Holt's gun was holstered; he'd needed both hands to climb.

"You did have me fooled, Mr. Holt, if that's any consolation." It was the pilgrim from back at the fork, all right. "I reckoned I had you pinned."

Holt's palms were bleeding a little from the friction of the fall. "Who are you?" he asked, to buy time.

"Lose the firepower," the man said.

Holt used two fingers to take the Colt from its holster. He tossed it so it landed halfway between them.

"Name's Jackson. You heard of me?"

"Sure," Holt lied.

"There was a time you would have," Jackson said contemplatively. "Them shots, then, they was from your woman. Where is she?"

Holt sat up straighter and gestured with his head to Jackson's right. "She's right there," Holt said. "I'll be goddamned."

Jackson read something in his voice that told him Holt was pulling no trick, and glanced quickly over his shoulder. Sam was a dozen paces behind him, holding her .38 in both hands as Holt had taught her. "Me, too," Jackson said.

He stayed out of Holt's reach as he retrieved Holt's gun, then moved to a position where he could see them both. "You gonna shoot me, little miss?"

"I might," Sam said. "And I'm not little."

Jackson shook his head in an if-that-don't-beat-all gesture—and brought up his gun.

Holt hollered, "No!"

Sam gasped and shot Jackson in the right thigh.

Jackson dropped his own and Holt's weapon to grab at his leg. Holt lunged, caught him around the knees and dragged him down, then snatched up the Colt and put it in his face. Jackson froze. Holt got the other gun, rose and stepped back.

No one moved for a few moments, until Sam turned and kicked angrily at a pebble and let the gun drop from her fingers. "Pick it up," Holt snapped, "and keep it aimed between this jasper's eyes."

She did. She was mostly okay, and Holt wanted her to stay that way.

To no one in particular, Jackson said, "I used to be someone. I brought in near forty thousand dollars worth of bad men, some of them facedown across their saddles."

"Good for you," Holt said harshly.

"Put most of the money into a ranch on the Virgin River, and did pretty good, too," Jackson went on, as if working this out in his mind. "But when I run into you, I figured why not one more for old time's sake." He looked Holt up and down, as if searching for pity in one of Holt's pockets. "I reckon all that cow-growing made me lose my touch." Jackson examined the blood bubbling from his leg. "Jeez but it hurts getting shot."

"I know," Holt said. "Listen up."

Jackson tried and failed to stand, sunk back onto the sand. Holt worked on organizing his thoughts. Uptrail a ways the bay and the roan were nuzzling a third horse, Jackson's no doubt. Sam watched the ex–bounty hunter with something like fascination, her distress under control.

"I can kill you quick," Holt said to Jackson, "or I can leave you unhorsed and you can die slow. Third alternative, I can bind your wound and you can ride on home. The bullet go all the way through?"

"Yeah, but it broke my leg bone." Jackson gave Holt a reproachful look. "I bet I never walk right again."

"You've walked enough, old man," Holt said savagely. He hated the idea that the son of bitch had tried to kill him.

"I'll take that third alternative," Jackson said.

Their shadows were growing longer, although night chill was hours away, and Holt was growing increasingly thirsty, not to mention weary. In the middle distance a hawk caught an updraft and circled on motionless wings. "I assume there's paper on me," Holt said. "How much?"

"Three thousand."

It was too much. Someone wanted him badly, and Holt had three guesses who. "Alive or dead?" he asked.

Jackson managed a smile. "According to the poster," he said, "any which way is fine."

It was five o'clock by the time they got Jackson patched up enough so he wouldn't bleed to death, and boosted horseback heading down the trail in the opposite direction. Holt left him with the promise that if Jackson mentioned this encounter or any clue to Holt's whereabouts, Holt would come looking for him, but they both knew this was an idle threat. On the other hand, Jackson had no good motive for talking, and reason not to: He'd be facing a deal of ridicule, without there being any money in it for him.

Still, it was not a gamble Holt would have taken on willingly, and he was brooding on this when Sam, ahead of him on the track, reined up and said, "My Lord."

Holt rode up beside her. They'd crested the pass, and the sight on the other side was admittedly astonishing.

A half mile ahead and a hundred feet below was a huge oval of garden carved from sere wilderness, at least a mile wide at its narrowest diameter. Around its rim a post-and-pole fence demarked a boundary between fecundity and the desert's desolation as abruptly as a line some kid might draw with a stick in the sand.

Within were rings. The outermost arc was a sea of tall green grass dotted here and there with haymows from the first cutting. Maybe a hundred pairs of cows and calves grazed it, along with several dozen horses, and five polled bulls were penned in a feed lot. The next curving band was a swatch of fields lush with mature grain, corn, truck crops, and an orchard.

It enclosed the town proper, which had been laid out with evident thought to municipal planning. A decent-sized creek bisected the oval the long way, paralleled by two main streets. Boardwalk-fronted commercial establishments lined the far side of each street, with the creek side left as open space. The streets' ends were connected with wagon bridges to form a rectangle, and bound at the middle by a smaller arched footbridge. Side lanes spoked out to a ring road running along the inside of the gardens, dotted with five dozen neat cottages.

A mile upstream twin drop gates flanked the creek, heading two broad ditches that couldn't have been dug more than three years earlier, judging from the height of the willow and cottonwood that had begun to take root on the two canals' banks. When the ditches reached the edge of the pasture, they branched and went on branching, carrying water throughout the compound in an intricate system of tributaries.

Holt had never seen the likes. There was even a watering pond amidst one of the fields where a ditch pooled.

"Golem," Sam confirmed.

"That water looks damned sweet. Let's get us some." After he'd slaked his immediate thirst, he meant to treat the secondary with a few belts of whatever hootch was available in this town.

"Hold on a second," Sam said. "I think I know the answer but I want to be clear on this. Why can't we go after Fitzsimmons or Stringer or Pert?"

Holt studied the pretty little village. "Best of circumstances, it would be their word against mine, and each has lots more pull than me. But this isn't the best of circumstances; now that we're officially wanted, they can jail us before we get a chance to say a word."

"What makes the Big Man a better bet?"

"He's the only bet I've got," Holt said. "He can tell me which of the three I'm really after."

"Knowledge is power," Sam said.

"That's a thought."

"I didn't frame it. Francis Bacon."

"He write for your magazine?"

"Not likely. He died in 1626."

Holt raised his eyes heavenward. "I was kidding. I'm not a complete idiot."

"That's nice to know," Sam said, not unkindly. "So assuming we find him, how do you make the Big Man go along with your plan?"

"I twist him somehow, get the goods on him for other bad stuff, or maybe just beat on him. Unlike the others, he can't get me into any more trouble than I'm already in."

"Face-to-face, he could be hazardous to your health," Sam said.

"Isn't that a cheering thought." Holt thumped the gelding's flanks with his boot heels. "Let's go to town," he said.

CHAPTER
EIGHT

To Holt's satisfaction, Golem boasted a handsome saloon at the head of the near main street by which he and Sam entered town. Next door was a hardware store and a photography studio, and at the end of the street a livery. Opposite these businesses, the creek bank had been seeded with grass, and about the footbridge, people on blankets were taking the sun after the workday's end.

The paid no little attention to Holt and Sam, although he divined no hostile purport to their gazes and chalked it up to the novelty of strangers. The kids wore homespun shirts and denim britches held up with suspenders, while the women were mostly in long black frocks.

Holt reined up at the hitching post in front of the saloon. A hand-painted sign, nicely done, said this was the Pishon House.

"I'll see to the horses," Holt said. "Make sure you get down plenty of water, first order of business."

"You're thirsty, too."

"So are the animals," Holt said, "and you always want to see to them before yourself."

"I'll remember that," she said, not sarcastically.

He led her horse down to the stable, but when he dismounted and walked the mounts into the dimness beyond its high broad door, he found it empty of animals and men. Holt blinked as his eyes dilated. "Hello, the liveryman!" he called.

"Hello yourself," someone said behind him.

Holt turned as a figure emerged from one of the stalls

and came forward into what light the door admitted. "You the liveryman?"

"Who's asking?"

As Holt's eyes adjusted, he realized that his interlocutor stood no higher than his own chest. "The name is Herschel." The kid was maybe eleven, skinny and dressed in sweat-stained coveralls. "And yours?"

"Holt."

"What's the matter, can't afford a first name?" the kid said. "Give me a dollar."

"Why should I?"

"Money buys friendship." Herschel had thick dark hair and olive skin.

"Who taught you that?"

"Okay, don't give me a dollar," the kid said. "Maybe you already got all the friends you need."

Another figure appeared in the shadows. "Give him the dollar. It can't hurt."

Holt forked over. Herschel took his horse to a stall and ducked beneath the gelding's belly to undo the cinch.

The other figure came closer. "See how you benefit when you are trusting?" he cautioned.

"So you are the liveryman," Holt tried.

The man gestured with a pitchfork whose tines were stained with manure. "Certainly not," he said. "I'm just fond of shoveling horseshit."

Holt halfway thought he might not be kidding, because this man didn't look like any stable hand he had ever run into. He was around thirty, with handsome, intelligent features, curly black hair, and a thin torso incongruous with the muscle his work had layered onto his arms and shoulders. He wore low-cut boots and canvas slacks. "What can I do for you?"

"Put up me and my partner's horses?" Holt inquired.

The liveryman looked around elaborately. "I believe I can make room."

"Grain 'em and rub 'em down."

"Seventy-five cents a day," the liveryman said. "Two-day minimum."

Holt found three dollars of Sam's money, and the liveryman stuffed the bills in his pocket without counting them. "My name is Robert Lerner," he said presently. "And you're . . . ?"

"This hombre who wants his horses seen to."

Lerner smiled nicely. "Here's where, in the usual course of things, I'm supposed to say, 'We don't get many strangers in Golem,' and after that, 'What brings you to town?' "

Holt prepared to demonstrate a certain amount of irritation.

"But I won't," Lerner continued. "Maybe later."

Herschel returned to lead Sam's horse toward the stalls. When the roan tossed its head, he jerked it back down and at the same time murmured softly. "The kid knows his horses," Holt said to Lerner.

"I am teaching him the trade."

"He your son?"

Lerner shook his head. "I see to him. An act of charity." Lerner smelled of gin. "Do you endorse charity, sir?"

"This is the first livery I've been in a fellow had to pass a test," Holt said.

Herschel was currying the roan. Lerner watched him with pride. "He'll take to you," Lerner said.

"Why's that?" Holt hadn't the slightest idea what they were talking about.

"He will see you as what I am not."

That cleared up nothing. "Everyone has got to believe in something," Holt said tartly. "I believe I will get a drink."

The kid stepped aside while Holt untied his saddlebags and Sam's, but he stared up at Holt with wide eyes that presently descended to take in Holt's gun. "You might want to teach me to shoot," the kid said.

"I might not," Holt said, "and what for?"

"A man has got to know how to shoot," Herschel said.

"Swell." Holt slung one pair of bags over each shoulder. "Look me up when you grow into a man."

Lerner was staring at him with a faint smile. Holt ignored him and carried his burden out into the desert sunlight.

The saloon held a half-dozen round tables, each with four or five straight-backed chairs. The bar was hardwood with a brass rail, and inset in the ornately carved back bar were mirrors that reflected an usually large variety of bottles and pyramids of thick-bottomed glasses. A chandelier, its candles unlit, hung above the room's center. Against a side wall a stairway ascended to a second floor.

Holt found Sam at a table in the far corner from the bar, beneath a little stage that held an upright piano. He flopped the saddlebags on the floor and sat. On the table was a pitcher of water and a couple of glasses. Holt poured, drained the glass, and refilled it. Sam was eating something dark and roughly round.

"Pickled pig's foot?" Holt asked.

Sam laughed. "You see any pigs when we rode in? These people are Jewish, Holt."

"All of them?" He sipped at the water.

Sam nodded. "They don't eat pork."

"I don't know much about Jewish people." For clientele the saloon had four men playing cards across the room, and two more propped against the bar, talking with the tavern keeper.

Each was dressed the same, in a black frock coat, black trousers, and a brimmed black hat with rounded crown, and each was clean-shaven except for long curly sideburns. "Anybody say anything?" Holt asked Sam, his voice low and cautious.

"To me? Yeah, the bartender said, 'Can I help you?' " She gestured with what she was gnawing on. "It's a turkey gizzard. Not bad."

Holt felt fidgety. "I'm going to have me a drink. You want something?"

Beside her water was a stein glazed with beer foam. "Another of these, thanks."

The other patrons watched Holt when he went to the bar, but with expressions neutral as the bartender's tone when he said, "What'll it be?" The bartender wore the same clothes and facial hair as his customers.

Holt paid forty cents for two beers and a shot of bourbon for himself; at least they didn't gouge the tourists in this town. Back at the table he said, "They're kind of strange."

"They're not *strange*, Holt, they're different. It's a bad habit to generalize about people you are not accustomed to."

"All right," Holt grumbled. He dug out his makings and went to work on cigarettes. "What kind of a name is Pishon House? Wasn't the Pishon the first river in the Garden of Eden?"

It was Sam's turn to look surprised.

"The Bible was my primer when my mother taught me to read," Holt explained, feeling a little self-satisfied. "I still don't get the name, though."

"River," Sam said. "Water."

"Watering hole," Holt figured out. "That's pretty clever." Sam took the cigarette he offered. "Jewish people are."

"Who's generalizing now?" Holt needled.

A match appeared in front of Sam's face. She looked up, nodded pleasantly, and leaned forward to accept the light.

Lerner, the liveryman, was standing by the table. He grinned at Holt. "You want to ask me to join you?"

"Why should I?"

Lerner was wearing a shirt now, and from its breast pocket he took a sheet of paper folded in fours, opened it, and dropped it before Holt. Herschel had appeared behind Lerner and was trying to peer around him. "Go play," Lerner ordered.

Holt unfolded the paper. It was the poster on Holt that Jackson had mentioned, except Jackson had left out that Sam's picture was on it, too, above the figure of two thousand dollars—five thousand in all for both of them.

Lerner took a chair without waiting further to be asked. "I guess now is the time for my lines." His grin broadened.

"We don't get many strangers in Golem," Lerner pronounced in a stagy manner. "What brings you to town?"

Lerner was on his second gin, beefing up the scent Holt smelled in the livery. Holt sipped another bourbon, for which Lerner had paid. That and the fact that Sam seemed to want to hear Lerner's story was all that was keeping a lid on Holt's temper.

"You look edgy and a little fatigued," Lerner said. "I'd prescribe one more drink and then a good night's sleep."

Holt had so far volunteered only that he was innocent of the murder that led to his incarceration in Yuma and that he and Sam were seeking a very large man who they had reason to believe was in the vicinity of Golem. "What are you, a doctor?" Holt asked unkindly.

Lerner worked on his gin. "Was," Lerner said. "Long ago and far away."

"I reckon your specialty is equine disorders."

Sam dropped her cigarette butt on the plank floor and ground it out under her boot heel. "There's this thing reporters come to know," she said to Holt. "You rarely learn anything listening to yourself."

Lerner's order to Herschel to "go play" turned out to be literal: The kid was at the piano, caressing the keys to elicit a soft tune that Holt did not recognize. "I'm teaching him piano as well as husbandry," Lerner said.

"Fine," Holt said. "What about this doctoring business?"

"I had a practice in Newport, Rhode Island. They've got wonderful gin there." Gin and memory softened Lerner's gaze. "Lovely women, too. One of the lovely women was my secretary. Hair blond as butter. A *shiksa*."

"What's he saying?" Holt demanded of Sam.

"The girl wasn't Jewish."

Lerner nodded. "When my wife discovered us, she took everything—my money, my son, my dog, and my secretary. They're all living together in Saint Louis." Lerner studied the dregs of his gin as a fortune teller studies tea leaves. "I miss that dog."

Holt had not eaten since breakfast, and the liquor was going to his head. He'd been guilty of a few precipitous acts fueled by drink, and considered the wisdom of taking either a meal or a nap.

The saloon door's bat wings swung open to admit a tall, imposing middle-aged man. He wore the same somber dress and facial hair as the other men, except that his curly sideburns blended into a full salt-and-pepper beard. He carried himself with ominous authority.

He held out a palm to Lerner, and the liveryman/doctor retrieved the wanted poster from his pocket. The tall man showed it to Holt without unfolding it. "You've seen this already, I believe," he said.

Holt smiled up at the tall man, got his legs under him, lunged across the table, got hold of Lerner's shirtfront and said, "You little squealing son of a bitch."

"Please don't," the tall man said.

Herschel stopped his tune, and in the pregnant silence Holt looked around. The two men at the bar held guns leveled on him. Although they did not seem comfortable with the pose, Holt wasn't ready to make an issue of it. He released Lerner reluctantly.

The imposing man went around the table and took the last chair. "My name is Mordecai Reich," he said. "Rabbi Reich, if you prefer. And you . . ."

"Are in deep shit," Holt finished for him.

Reich stroked his beard. "That's up to you."

"How so?" Holt settled back; guns were still on him.

Reich studied Holt. "Are you a man of violence?"

"Not generally." Holt indicated the folded poster in Reich's hand. "I didn't kill that woman, for example."

"Nonetheless, I could arrest you both," Reich pointed out, "and be richer for it."

Through the saloon's mullioned windows Holt could see women and children on the creek bank folding up their blankets, and beyond them the storefronts on the other street: a bank, feed and grain, café, and what looked to be a church. The scene was tranquil and, to Holt, jarring.

"What do you want, Mr. Reich?" Sam cut in.

Reich did not acknowledge the question. "On the other hand," he said to Holt, "you could ride out of Golem a free man, the way you rode in, and with money in your pocket."

Holt stared into Reich's dark eyes. "How much money?"

"One thousand dollars."

"Who do I have to kill?" Holt was growing weary of taking the defensive.

"No one who doesn't deserve to die." Reich played with his beard some more. "You have your problem, and I have mine."

"Fine," Holt snapped impatiently. "Let's keep them to ourselves."

"It's not that simple." Reich gazed past Holt to his men. "Hear me out or I will have you arrested."

"I'm listening," Holt said. "What is it you want?"

"Your help?" Reich suggested.

Holt finished his bourbon. "Tell your tale, Rabbi."

CHAPTER NINE

The word for Golem, Holt decided, was "spruce." Rarely had he encountered a village so well-fashioned and tidily kept up, from the sturdy construction and clean lines of the buildings to the unrutted main streets and filigree trim on the footbridge. As he followed Reich, Holt saw that even the creek had been neatened. It was channeled through town so it flowed smooth as a canal, and the banks, built up into levees, were riprapped with round river stones.

Holt expected the café on the far bank to have a cute name like the saloon, but the sign above the canopy of its boardwalk said only *Bea's Restaurant*, in cursive letters painted by someone with a sure hand. The interior was well-lit but cool, and business was good. Family folk occupied round tables of the same sort as in the bar. The plank flooring was clean-swept, and along one wall were booths, benches with high backs fronting counter tables, with salt and pepper shakers and places already set on mats. The walls were hung with framed oil paintings, some of desert landscapes, others of biblical tableaux.

The booths were filled up as well, except for the last and most private one, in the back corner. Reich led them to it, and something told Holt it was reserved for his pleasure. Before they were hardly settled, a waitress appeared. She was around eighteen, with long dark hair and a swelling bosom.

The waitress said, "Shalom, Reb," nodded pleasantly

to Holt and Sam, and set out cartes. Holt was nonplussed, and Sam caught his surprise. "It's called a menu," she teased.

"Places that get my custom," Holt said, "tend to have a chalkboard on the wall." He watched the waitress disappear through a swinging door beside a cutout window that emitted kitchen-type noises. "Or no bill of fare at all," Holt went on. "You know what they got because they've all got the same: Beefsteak, chicken-fried steak, mutton, or pork chop."

"I hope you didn't have your heart set on a pork chop," Sam said.

Holt looked up in time to catch a trace of a smile behind Reich's beard. She had that way, Holt learned in their time together, of getting on people's good sides, and he supposed it might come in handy now. He could learn from her a little about bending.

The menu listed the beefsteak, but also a bunch of items that were even more obscure than the stuff in a chop suey house: gefilte fish, knishes, and something called latkes. The waitress returned and Sam ordered kishka with gravy. "Steak with spuds on the side sounds good," Holt mumbled.

"For me as well," Reich told the waitress.

Holt could have used a shot of something while they were waiting, but since no one offered, he got out his makings instead. "Please don't," Reich said. *"Der kinder."*

"The children," Sam said.

"It is bad for them," Reich said.

"Bad for me, too." Holt put away the pouch. "You speak Jewish?" he said to Sam.

She shook her head no. "I had a little German in college, and in Yiddish that word is the same."

Holt had been wondering about Reich's accent. It was vaguely like that of the immigrants Holt had encountered in Lutheran church, but softer, less guttural.

Reich said, "Are you a prejudiced man, Mr. Holt?"

"I've been a peace officer most of my life," Holt said. "I had to deal with all sorts—spigs, greasers, Negroes, bohunks. I'd like to think I treated them all equal."

Holt didn't know why Sam was hiding a smile, because Reich seemed satisfied with his answer. "And you are a man who can handle himself in difficult . . . or let us say, dangerous, situations?"

"If I never found myself in a dangerous situation for the rest of my days, I'd die happy," Holt said. "But I don't guess that's what fate has got in mind for me."

The waitress dealt out plates. Holt's steak was good-sized and succulent with juice, except that instead of potatoes, the side dish was some kind of pancake. Holt went for his knife and fork, then noticed that Reich had bowed his head. Holt held steady, a bit embarrassed, while Reich said a prayer in yet another language, neither English nor Yiddish.

"First we will eat," Reich said when he was finished. "Business is best discussed on a full stomach."

The steak was as good as it looked, and when Holt tried the pancakes, he found they were made of potatoes after all, like hash browns glued together into a patty. But he was mystified by Sam's kishka, a stuffed ring of something with the gravy over it. When Sam finished the stuffing, she cut up the ring with her knife and went to work on it.

"Derma," she said in response to his unvoiced curiosity. "Stuffed cow intestine."

"Looks good," Holt said dryly.

"Want a taste?"

"Thanks," Holt said, "but no."

Reich smiled for the second time. Aren't we all getting along swell, Holt thought.

But eating good food had reminded him that he was hungry, and when the main course was done, he accepted the waitress's suggestion of peach pie. It arrived with cheese on the plate and coffee for all three of them, and the pie was good enough to sate Holt and give him almost cordial feelings toward Reich.

Holt had to admit that after their initial confrontation in the saloon, the man had been civil to him. When Reich led them up the staircase to the second floor, Holt was surprised to find four boarding rooms, two to either side of a narrow corridor. Reich installed them in adjacent accommodations, waiting while Holt tossed his saddlebags on the bed and Sam took somewhat longer doing whatever it was that women did behind closed doors.

Now, in the café, Reich said, "You may smoke."

In the course of their meal, the other citizens of Golem had finished up and left, and they had the place to themselves. The waitress returned simultaneously with the start of Holt's cigarette-building, deposited a glass ashtray and retreated.

"Let's figure I go along with whatever it is you want," Holt said to Reich, "and let's figure I can trust you."

"You can," Reich said.

"What's to say someone else in town isn't going to turn us in for the price on our heads?"

"You have my guarantee."

Holt handed the first smoke to Sam and lit it for her with a match he struck under the table's lip. "You pretty much run things in this town."

"I made Golem," the rabbi declared.

Holt poured tobacco flakes into a second creased paper. "Time for your story, I suspect."

Reich spoke in a low, measured tone, and Holt found himself drawn into the tale to the extent that when his cigarette burned to a stub, he ground it out and didn't roll another.

A half-dozen years earlier, Reich said, he had been a man of substance. In addition to his rabbinical duties, he was owner of a thriving textile manufactory in Lowell,

Massachusetts. Still, his life was a constant upstream swim against a tide of bigotry to which he and other members of his Orthodox Jewish community were subject. Ultimately, he became fed up; he liquidated his substantial business, convinced his congregants that there remained in this country places where men and women could live unmolested, and organized them into an emigrant company. At the railhead in St. Louis, Reich purchased wagons and supplies and engaged scouts and a trail boss. On a bright spring day, the party headed west.

"I sense that you are a man of wit, if not of formal education," Reich said as they smoked. "You've observed the results of our husbandry."

"You've built a fine town," Holt concurred. "Homestead Act?"

"Yes." The law provided a half-section of federal land free for the taking to any settler who worked and occupied it for three years. "We proved up our claims early this year, and the congregation has chosen to hold the grants communally," Reich continued. "The arrangement has maintained without rancor. More importantly, we've built up a herd of beeves, sufficient that soon we will be ready to make our first drive to market."

"Something is getting in your way," Holt said. "Mormons would be my guess."

"Correct, Mr. Holt," Reich said, "and that is why I need your help."

Reich knew the townsite he chose for Golem was inside the Utah Territory, he went on, but his people had the legal right to homestead it, and he also hoped that, since the Mormons had been driven to the desert by religious persecution, they would be sympathetic to others similarly oppressed.

Reich was right to a degree. During the colony's first winter, Golem was visited by a delegation led by one of the Council of Twelve, and the confrontation was cordial.

Now Reich wondered if that were not a sop, a sham predicated on a belief that Golem would fail miserably. But as Holt could see now—and as others realized—the town was destined, as Reich put it, to "become fruitful and multiply."

The previous autumn the atmosphere turned chilly. The Golemites were busy with gelding, breeding, and stacking the third cutting of hay when Elder Lemuel Baynes appeared in a black one-horse shay, accompanied by six riders.

Reich knew of his neighbor. On several occasions cows from Baynes's herd had wandered to Golem, where they'd stand at the fence and gaze hungrily at the thick grass within. Reich dispatched men to drive the strays home; they reported Baynes was running nearly five hundred head on both hay and open range in the next valley about ten miles distant, and that his home place was large and bespoke prosperity. However, neither they nor Reich had ever met Baynes himself face-to-face.

Baynes's six-man honor guard did not strike Reich as cowhands. They were armed and wore hard looks, and their eyes darted warily as the Golem field workers gathered around. Their leader was a thick, broad man with a belly that lopped over his gun belt and mustachioed face under a derby hat he wore low enough to obscure his eyes.

Baynes was tersely polite: He wished to expand his holdings, and to that end meant to buy the buildings, lands, and stock of Golem. He offered $100,000 cash money.

It would take the collective forty years to see that kind of income, but when Reich presented the proposal to his congregation, the rejection was nearly unanimous. The sole dissenter was Robert Lerner, and Reich suspected that he was merely being iconoclastic for the mischief of it.

Reich conveyed the decision by letter to Baynes, and

hoped the matter was closed, although the fact that Baynes had come with those six armed men troubled him. Baynes surely had not felt the need for protection, which meant the men represented a subtle show of force.

The winter was mild and nearly snowless, and the beeves not only maintained weight, but grew fatter. By May the land was once again verdant, and the circle of fields enclosing Golem was dotted with cows nursing wobbly-legged calves.

On a sun-streaked morning late in that month, the riders and their derby-hatted leader reappeared. Baynes wished Reich to come to him.

"Lemuel," Holt mused in the café. "Wasn't he the king in Proverbs who cautioned against strong drink?"

"A perfect name for a Mormon, would you not agree?" Reich said sardonically. "In Hebrew, it means 'dedicated to the Lord.'"

Holt noticed Herschel lurking by the café door, careful to stay at Reich's back.

"I resented Baynes's imperious demand for an audience," Reich said to Holt and Sam, "but I went because I wished to know as much as I could about the man and his intentions."

"And his intentions were?" Holt asked, toying with his coffee cup.

"To have this land," Reich said, "by hook or by crook."

Baynes was frank: The Council of Twelve in Salt Lake City, the ruling Elders of the Church of Latter Day Saints, would no longer countenance the presence of the Jewish community. Reich could either accept Baynes's offer—which he now reduced to eighty thousand—or Golem could face unspecified consequences.

Reich asked for and received two weeks to think about it, but that was a ruse. In fact, he spent the first couple days of the grace period sobering up Lerner, and then dispatched him to Salt Lake City, choosing him because Lerner was, after him, the most learned and sophisticated man in town.

The news he brought back was only mildly encouraging. Baynes had lied: The Elders had no intention of supporting Baynes's campaign to purge the Golemites. Utah had been a territory for twenty-five years, and while the council wished in the best of worlds that it would remain exclusively Mormon, they realistically accepted the impossibility of that ambition. More important to them was that Utah remain civilized and unsullied in the eyes of the rest of the nation. The Church was still smarting from the negative impact of the Meadow Mountains Massacre of 1857, when, in a fit of anti-Gentile hysteria, a company of Mormon militia slaughtered 120 non-Mormon emigrants.

Further, Baynes was what was known as a jack Mormon, an apostate who had broken with the main Church by rejecting its teachings on plural marriages. Lerner heard rumor that Baynes had four wives.

But Baynes, by dint of his wealth and his six-man army, also had power, and a certain leverage over the council. So while the council might even be moderately sympathetic to Golem's plight, it refused to enter into the conflict.

Lerner uncovered one further tidbit, by luck rather than savvy. The night before he was to depart Salt Lake, he fell off the wagon and joined a poker game in a back alley blind pig, a sub-rosa saloon. In the game's course, he happened to describe the man in the derby hat, who turned out to be known to one of the other players. His name was Cavan, and he carried a reputation.

"I've heard of him," Holt said in the café. "Hired gun who's supposed to have busted a few banks. He rode through when I was sheriffing in Grand Junction. One large, mean Harp."

"From County Cavan, I assume," Sam said.

"Actually he's from Limerick. We had a conversation, and reached the point of agreeing that his best move would be to ride on down the trail." To Reich, Holt said, "What did you do when the two weeks were up?"

"I convinced the people that we must stand our ground." Reich stared at the tabletop. "Now I see the error of my ways."

The comment and the miserable expression that accompanied it gave Holt pause. "How's that?"

"The Lord moves in mysterious ways, and chooses His agents arcanely," Reich said. "He does not want us in this place, and Baynes was delivering His judgment."

"What are you blathering on about?" Holt snapped.

The pretty dark-haired girl refilled their coffee cups. Reich waited until she had gone. "The name of this town," he said. "How do you think it came to me?"

"I've got no idea," Holt said, "but I guess I'm about to find out."

Reich evinced no reaction to his sarcasm. "A vision from Jehovah," he said. "A vision that has come true."

"A golem is an automaton," Sam explained. "An artificial human."

"Some kind of monster?" Holt asked.

"Maybe," Sam said significantly, "or a large man masquerading as a monster."

Reich shook his head. "This is a golem for true."

"Who's seen him?" Holt put in.

"I told you about the one I talked to," Sam said, "Solomon Stein."

"He and his family have left," Reich said. "Two others have followed, and soon more will depart, including I myself."

Holt felt more indignant than angry; over the course of the story, he had come to develop some sympathy for Mordecai Reich. "That's crazy. There's no such thing as ghosts and monsters."

"All is possible from the Lord's hand," Reich said. "I

am a man of education and rationality, but I am also a man of God and I respect His works, beneficent and malevolent. 'The earth shook and trembled; the foundations of heaven moved and shook, because He was angry,' " Reich quoted.

"Second Samuel," Holt cited impatiently. "What's gotten you into this state?"

"The terror of His wrath," Reich said mournfully.

To Holt the cause and effect seemed obvious and unconnected to any supernatural mumbo-jumbo, given that the mutilations began three days after Baynes's ultimatum ran out. A bull was gelded, and cows were found with their udders severed. These incidents, each involving a single animal, had occurred on average two or three times each fortnight in the last two months since Baynes delivered his threat, Reich said.

"You think about posting guards?" Holt demanded.

"At first we did, but the golem eluded them," Reich said. "Stein was not a guard, but an insomniac who was taking a nocturnal walk and encountered the apparition by happenstance. All his tale accomplished was to put an end to anyone volunteering for sentry duty." Reich made a dismissive gesture. "Except for Robert Lerner."

Lerner, Holt decided, was a more complex ball of wax than he'd first given him credit for. "Did Lerner ever spot him?"

"Yes," Reich said, "and what he saw froze him on the spot. Thank the Lord the golem did not perceive him. Lerner watched while the golem disemboweled one of our fattest steers."

Holt drew a deep sigh. "Look, Rabbi," he said, "I fear God as much as the next hombre, but you've got to figure that Baynes is behind these mutilations, and that your golem is a natural man."

"I don't," Reich said frankly, "but I wish you to prove me wrong. Find this man, if he is such, and stop him."

Reich stared from dark eyes sunk deep within their sockets. "Will you do it?"

Holt answered the question with a question. "Do I have a choice?"

CHAPTER
TEN

Herschel was doodling at the piano in the saloon, but paying more attention to Lerner. The liveryman was studying the hands of a poker game at the table below the little stage, and judging from his stack of chips, wasn't doing too badly. Lerner folded, and Holt watched the man to his left deal five-card stud. Lerner bluffed wired aces from the first round, dropped the last player at the fourth, and then flipped his hole card to reveal an ace-jack bust.

Holt placed a hand on Lerner's shoulder as he raked in the pot. "Take a break," Holt said. "I'll buy you a drink."

The other players included a few of those who had drawn down on Holt earlier, but they regarded him with equanimity. That seemed to cinch Reich's promise that on the rabbi's say-so, Holt would be safe for the time being from anyone trying to deliver him for the bounty.

"I never turn down a drink." Lerner dry-washed his surgeon's hands. "I'm going to take ten, gentlemen."

At the bar Lerner ordered gin and a short beer back. Holt had bourbon, Sam a beer. As Holt went to work on smokes for the three of them, Herschel popped up at his elbow. "You want to roll one of them for me?"

Holt gave the kid a look and got a gap-toothed grin in response. Herschel put a finger close to Holt's gun without touching it. "How many notches you got on that?"

"The floor could use some work," Lerner said.

"I'd rather have a smoke," Herschel said.

"What you'll get," Lerner said, "is the back of my hand." He did not sound drunk, nor did he sound very menacing. Herschel laughed and went into the back room, emerging a moment later with a mop. "He swamps in exchange for use of the piano," Lerner explained. "His name is Vincent."

Holt could not get used to the quick switchbacks onto which Lerner's conversations veered. Sam merely rolled her eyes heavenward.

"I found him in the livery two summers back, helping himself to my tucker," Lerner explained. "He'd been on a wagon train to California, but he walked off; in fact, he'd been walking for three days."

"Why?" Sam asked.

"He won't say. Maybe his people beat him, maybe they were in some sort of desperate straits. All he told me was that his name was Vincent, which I imagine means his people were Italian. One Mediterranean race is as good as another, so I turned him into Herschel, which made him Jewish." Lerner shrugged. "Go figure."

Herschel finished his mopping and went back to the piano. Lerner drank his shot of gin and signaled the bartender for another. "Did you know that the rate of alcoholism is very low among Jews?"

"How do you fit into that?" Holt said.

Lerner indicated the poker table and his impressive pile of chips. "Could be it's a pose I find handy," he said. "Could be I don't drink nearly as much as I pretend to."

Herschel began to play. "Chopin," Sam said, half to herself. "Polonaise in G. Minor. He was younger than Herschel when he published it."

Lerner lowered his voice confidentially, went on to Holt: "Could be I'm a good guy to have on your side."

Holt lit a cigarette and passed it to him. "Enough couldbes. Tell me about this golem."

Lerner blew out smoke. "Giganticism."

Holt waited for him to go on, but it was Sam who picked up the thread. "A birth disorder of the endocrinal system. The signs are abnormal growth, scaling of the skin, and a distortion of facial bone structure, so the victim looks almost like a Neanderthal."

Holt gaped at her. "Is there anything you *don't* know?"

"How to make your horse stop blowing when you're trying to cinch a saddle," she said readily. "Maybe you could show me."

She'd had four beers over the course of the evening, and it struck Holt that she was moving toward coquettish. "You think this golem is a giant?" he asked Lerner.

"I never encountered a victim in my practice, but when I saw him, it triggered some memory from medical school, and I looked it up. I've still got some of my books."

"When was the last mutilation?"

"Maybe three weeks ago."

Holt considered, then smiled nicely at Sam. "Getting late. You must want to hit the sack."

"Sure do," Sam said briskly, "and what else is on your mind?"

Holt drew on his cigarette and frowned at the rising smoke.

"Because whatever it is, I'm going along," Sam continued.

He didn't see much chance of dissuading her, so he turned back to Lerner. "You drunk now?"

"No."

"You got a gun?"

"Yeah, and I know how to use it, if that was your next question."

"Why don't you fetch it," Holt suggested, "and after that we can take a stroll out to the pasture."

The desert night was cool and clear, and the great wash of the Milky Way arched overhead as Lerner opened a gate in the pasture's inner fence ring. Knee-deep grass brushed Holt's trouser legs, and he could hear the ripple of the irrigation ditches. Fat cows slept in lumpen mounds. Though the moon was new, the stars brightened the evening so brilliantly that Holt could see the opposite fence.

It was unlikely they'd run into the Big Man that night. It would be too great a piece of luck, and Holt had not been feeling lucky lately. Indeed, the back of his mind held the nagging apprehension that this adventure was not destined to pay off. Could be this Big Man was not the one who'd framed him; could be he didn't exist, that what they were dealing with here was mass hysteria. Hell, Holt thought peevishly, maybe he really *was* a ghost.

"Looked like you were ahead of the game when we pulled you from the table," Sam said to Lerner.

"I generally win," Lerner said, not bragging. "People figure drunks for fools and get careless. Do you play?"

Sam feigned surprise. "Poker isn't for women, Mr. Lerner."

"Robert," Lerner corrected. "Are you trying to duck my question?"

"I've played once or twice, for matchsticks," Sam said. "I'm sure I'd be shark bait for a player like you."

Lerner smiled. "You're lying, right?"

"Right," Sam said, smiling back. "Maybe I'll sit in at your table after all."

"Maybe I'll keep one hand on my pocketbook."

Holt's primary purpose was to get a closer look at the lay of the land, and what he saw was perplexing. The haymows provided the only cover, and they were spaced far enough apart so a man would have to expose himself plenty to get to one of them. "Reich said there was guards for a time, but it didn't do any good."

"That's right," Lerner said. "No one but me and Stein ever saw him, and the butcherings went right on, guard or no guard."

"How'd he keep out of sight?" Holt wondered.

"Maybe golems can make themselves invisible," Lerner said sardonically.

Holt pondered. "Reich also said they happened every three days or so," he went on after a time, "but you said it's been more like three weeks since the last one."

"I remember, because it was the night before the first cutting," Lerner said.

"Meaning there's a good chance the Big Man is long gone," Holt said.

"No reason for him to hang around," Lerner said. "If he was working for Baynes—and I'm certainly willing to buy into that notion—he did his job."

Holt worked to put his finger on something. "The hay came in late this year?"

"With the mild winter, the snowpack up in the mountains was down," Lerner explained, "and the creek ran lower than usual, so we couldn't irrigate as much as we'd've liked. Also, May and June were hot." He bent to pluck a blade of grass, which he stuck in the corner of his mouth. "It's cooled some and the creek's held steady. We'll get a second cutting, at least."

They crossed a tiny log bridge over a ditch. Holt kept them away from the haymows and his head moving. Objectively, it was a most unlikely spot for an ambush, but subjectively, all this golem talk gave him the creeps. "It doesn't strike me that you've got a lot of friends hereabouts," Holt said. "Why do you stay?"

"Where is there to go?" Lerner said. "Anyway, the kid needs me."

A cow lumbered to its feet, gazed in their direction incuriously, farted, and moseyed toward the ditch. "Why did Reich tell me the attacks were continuing?" Holt asked.

"That's the point I was about to make," Lerner said. "Reich wants to believe they're not over."

"That doesn't make sense," Sam said.

"Neither does the fact that he's caved in to Baynes," Lerner said. "Reich is ready to sell out, and he's been trying to convince the others. A lot of them had come over to his side by the fourth killing, but then they got their hopes up when the predations appeared to stop. At this point, I'd say the town's split fifty-fifty. Reich can be pretty persuasive." Lerner smiled again. "But then again, so can I."

"You've been going head-to-head with Reich?"

"Fix me a smoke, would you?" Lerner requested. When Holt hesitated, he said, "I'm not going to set anything on fire."

They were well away from the dried hay, and the night was windless, so Holt got out his makings.

"I may be the runt of the litter in this burg," Lerner said feistily, "but I love Golem and what these people have done here. I've been arguing that we're facing a man, not a spirit, a man who can be stopped if we all agree to do the job."

Holt handed over the cigarette and lit it with a match cupped in his palms. "That's fine," he said. "I got to admit to having developed a little grudging respect myself. But this present business is still twisted as a corkscrew."

"How so?" Sam asked.

Holt jerked a thumb in Lerner's direction. "It was this hombre who matched our faces with that wanted poster, and him that brought it to Reich's attention." He turned to Lerner. "Was it also you who suggested he force us to do this job?"

"That's right," Lerner said calmly.

"I'm going to accept that you've got an emotional attachment to this place and that's reason enough for you to want to stop Baynes's takeover attempt," Holt said. "For now, that will stand as the reason you fingered me." Holt thought. "But it doesn't fit with Reich going along with your plan, if you and he are at loggerheads."

"I wondered about that myself, although from the start, my hunch was that he would." Lerner blew out smoke. "Three possibilities."

Lerner counted off on his fingers. "One, Reich is a truly pious man. A part of him is honestly convinced that your Big Man is a golem and that he is cursed by God."

"What's God got against him?"

"We Jews," Lerner said wryly, "always figure God's on the lookout for some excuse to nail us, or even no excuse at all."

"Like Job," Holt said. "Get to the point."

"In Reich's case, God may have a good excuse after all," Lerner said. "As you heard, I have a way of nosing around. It turns out that mill back in Massachusetts that Reich made so much from, most of his workers were French Canadians—Catholics, of course—and until he saw the light, he treated them pretty poorly."

"Reich is a complex man," Sam opined.

"Exactly," Lerner concurred, "and his religious side conflicts with his intellect. Maybe he told you the truth, that he does want to be shown that his golem is a man, and he isn't cursed after all. But that's only the first possibility."

Lerner raised another finger. "Second alternative, he knows this golem business is a crock, and he's gone over to Baynes's side, probably for money."

"That's what I think," Sam said. "His sudden change of heart is suspicious."

Holt had been thinking. "I bet I can guess the third possibility, but I don't much like it."

Lerner nodded. "He's using you two as dogsbodies. Hiring you makes his congregation believe that he's doing something about the situation, but if you get too close to crossing him, he'll have you killed for the reward."

It was a pretty good divination of Holt's thoughts; maybe he had underestimated Lerner, as a man and as an ally. "What would you do, if you were me?"

Lerner burped. "Don't know." He hitched at his trousers. "What I'm going to do now, you'll excuse me, is tap a kidney."

Lerner wandered off into the dimness, working at the buttons of his fly. "I like him," Sam said to Holt. "You do, too, I'll bet."

"I keep learning new things about you," Holt said. "Now you're a mind reader." Holt could at least stand the failed doctor, but right now he had other fish to fry—such as the idea of riding out of this town immediately, under cover of the night. But he'd been doing a lot of running lately, foresaw more in his future, and for the moment was inclined to

accede to Mordecai Reich, against the chance it would lead
him to the Big Man.

But he didn't expect it to happen at that moment.

Holt saw Lerner disappear behind the nearest haymow to
do his business. A moment later Lerner let out a howl.

Holt drew his revolver as he moved toward the haystack,
snapping at Sam, "Stay put!" She didn't, of course; he
could hear her on his tail. Lerner shouted a second time,
but his voice was muffled.

Holt circled wide around the stack, was ten yards distant
when he caught sight of the extraordinary scene.

The Big Man held Lerner around the neck, so Lerner's
feet dangled above the tall grass. Lerner was making gur-
gling noises. To one side lay a cow, gutted from neck to
crotch, its entrails spilled and steaming in the night air.

Holt was bringing his gun up when Sam banged into
him. He stumbled and fired, a yard above the Big Man's
head.

The Big Man flung Lerner into the hay; Lerner flew a
good ten feet before he landed in its softness, although his
neck might already have been broken. In Holt's ear Sam
said urgently, "You can't kill him."

"I know that," Holt snapped. "I hadn't planned to."

Holt got to his knees. The Big Man was fleeing, and
Holt sighted on his legs below the thigh, using both hands.
He squeezed the trigger.

A moment before he fired, the Big Man disappeared.

Holt held steady. "What the hell?" he muttered. He got
to his feet, noted as he passed the haystack that Lerner was
moaning but stirring.

Behind him, Sam said, "Holt, get back here." She
sounded angry and frightened.

He advanced cautiously to the last place the Big Man
had been. The grass was crushed down, but there was no
other sign of him.

Holt backed away. The night was silent and nothing
moved. When he returned to the haystack, Lerner had made

it to his feet. He seemed whole, except that his voice was raspy when he said, "Jesus God."

"You all right?" Holt said.

"Hell no," Lerner got out. "He was going to kill me."

"Why didn't he?" Sam seemed the calmest of all of them.

"Maybe he specializes in cows," Holt said. But he knew that wasn't true; there was Sanchez, and Cat Lacey.

"It was him, wasn't it?" Sam said.

"It was him." Holt repictured the immense size, the lumbering gait; it was definitely the Big Man. "Where the hell did he go?" he asked.

But he had no answer, nor did Lerner or Sam. Lerner's voice at least was getting back to normal when he said, "You've got to get the son of a bitch, Holt."

"And then what?"

Lerner rested his hand on the butt of his gun. "I'll take care of the rest."

Holt felt his fear devolve into weariness. "We'll discuss that in the morning." He gazed around the vast, still pasture, his scan ending on the gutted cow. "Right about now," he said, "I could use some shut-eye."

CHAPTER
ELEVEN

Desert chaparral and bunchgrass were fragile, and minimal traffic would tromple down a trail through it. The one west out of Golem ran at first through flatland, but an hour out Holt saw hills rising ahead, not much more than five hundred feet high but steep-walled and foreboding as the day, which had dawned cloudy and gray with a hint of rain.

The heaviness of the air matched Holt's mood as he rode beside Sam. She had been going on for a while about an amusing incident in her early days as a reporter in the West. She'd sensed a story in a colorful hombre named Buckskin O'Brien, an old fraud who claimed to have partnered with everyone from John Colter to Bill Hickok. O'Brien did not think highly of modern times nor working women, so as a josh he took Sam out on a ride. Disappointed that she could sit a horse, he pulled out his jug and more or less challenged her to a drinking contest—except on her turns, Sam cheated. O'Brien passed out, and Sam had to wrestle him facedown onto the saddle to get him back to town. "Lucky he was an itty-bitty dried-up specimen," she said, "or I'd've had to leave him for the coyotes."

"Could you maybe quiet down for a bit?" Holt said. "I got things on my mind."

Sam flushed. "I beg your pardon, Holt. I forgot what a deep thinker you are."

He felt ashamed and a little dumb, because what he was mostly thinking about was her. He'd never ridden with a partner before, let alone a girl—he drew himself up mentally. He'd called her that once during their first days together, not meaning any offense. "Girls have pigtails and stand about yay high," she snapped. "The word you're searching for is 'woman.' "

Not that he minded having her at his side; it pleasured him no little, but it itched at him as well. Truth to tell, he did not know what to make of her—or perhaps more accurately, of the two of them together. When he tried to rationalize the situation, it made him glum. Samantha Lowell was of a different world, one he knew only from myth and hearsay that was likely distorted. The place from which she had come, physically and culturally, was as foreign to him as Mongolia.

Beyond all that, he felt some guilt at having involved her in his troubles. He tried to argue that his life depended on getting out of Yuma, but each time was drawn up short with the idea that a man took care of himself. Then he'd get angry, because now he was responsible for her.

But that wasn't right, either; Sam could take care of herself. Nor had she revealed a hint of resentment about becoming a fugitive. On the contrary, she seemed content with their situation, and content to be with him now. If that weren't enough, she was sweet, funny, and pretty, and he could think of no one else he wished at his side.

The low mountains loomed closer and the trail began to climb. Sam was brooding now, and Holt felt worse. *Hell, I've been with women.* Another mind-voice, *Sure you have—women like Cat Lacey.* But there was nothing wrong with Cat, except that like Holt himself, Cat existed in a different dimension from Sam.

Now Sam shot Holt a sharp glance, and he realized he had just sighed deeply. What was he telling himself? he wondered. That he was somehow her inferior, that he wasn't good enough for her?

He saw that this meandering trail of self-analysis was leading toward a marker post not so far distant, where he would seriously consider him and Sam coming together. The idea pleasured and frightened him. What had happened the previous night after the run-in with the Big Man wasn't much help in sorting out his feelings.

After they'd left Lerner and climbed to the rooms above the saloon, Holt said, "Well," and Sam said, "Hey."

Holt turned to face her. She looked concerned and sympathetic, and compellingly attractive in the dim light.

"He scares you, doesn't he?" she said. She meant the Big Man.

"Sure."

"But not enough to make you run," she went on. "I like the way you didn't hesitate a heartbeat when you knew he had Lerner." She kissed him on the cheek. "Sleep well."

He didn't. He tossed and turned and wrestled with his thoughts, and they were not of the Big Man.

"I did hesitate, though," Holt said as they rode up into the mountains.

"Did I miss the first part of this conversation?" Sam said stiffly.

Holt felt sheepish. "I'm sorry I snapped at you back there. I, um . . . I'm sorry," he finished lamely.

They were four hundred feet above the desert floor and a hundred yards from the pass that marked the boundary of Baynes's range, and the trail followed a deer track a yard wide. Holt dismounted and gathered the bay's reins. "We'll walk this part," he said.

Sam wasn't quite ready to accept his apology. "Why?"

On the downside edge the slope was almost a cliff. "It's easier on the horses," Holt said.

She snorted. "That's nonsense."

He felt the need to admit what he'd hidden on the bridge over the Colorado. "Heights bother me."

Her iciness melted in laughter. "You want me to hold your hand?" she asked, but she dismounted.

"Go ahead and make fun," Holt said. "Lots of people got fears—of cats, spiders, snakes, whatever. At least mine is rational." He gestured at the drop-off. "You fall here, you really will buy the ranch."

"You won't fall."

Holt led the bay along the shelf, careful not to look down. The horse took the passage with equanimity, and at its end they'd reached the crest. To Holt's relief, the other side was a more gentle descent. He remounted. Sam, who hadn't left the saddle, said, "Now that wasn't so bad."

"About hesitating," Holt said. "I was making a point."

"Okay." Whatever mad she'd taken on was gone. Another thing he liked: She was quick to anger but quick to let it go.

"Getting shot in the war," Holt went on, "it didn't only leave me with an achy back."

"I know," Sam interrupted. "You fear the next bullet will do the job. As long as you're quick enough, it won't."

"That's what I'm trying to tell you," Holt said, a little impatiently. "I've got this reluctance to pull my gun."

He expected her to tease or to tell him it was all in his mind—which he already knew—but when he looked up to take it, she was staring down the mountainside. All she said was, "Now might be a good time to get over it."

Holt followed her gaze. A couple hundred yards ahead at the foot of the descent, three men sat their horses. One was thick and big-bellied, and wore a derby hat.

Cavan and his two boys kept their hands folded casually but conspicuously on their saddle horns, and their expressions in faint smiles. As Holt and Sam rode up, Cavan said, "He's expecting you."

"How did you-all know we were coming?" Holt asked.

Cavan examined Holt. "You run me out of a town once."

Cavan's boys were of a type: too lean, weasel-eyed, and about three-quarters as tough as they thought they were. One said, "I guess we're just good at knowing stuff."

Or Mordecai Reich was a traitor, Holt thought; the rabbi'd had plenty of time to tip off Baynes.

"We'd best ride." Cavan grinned. "The great man awaits."

Within a mile they encountered free-range cattle, and soon after came upon irrigated fields and then a feed lot, where the best of Baynes's herd were being grained up for market. The trail widened to a track that passed under an arc of tangled antlers and continued toward a sprawling baronial mansion. The house rose two stories above a colonaded porch, and a spring creek ran through a truck garden to its side.

Elder Lemuel Baynes sat beneath the portico in a rocking chair, sipping at a tall glass of something cloudy.

Sam turned her horse so its flanks touched Holt's bay. "You'll want me to do most of the talking," she said in a low voice. Holt glared. "It's what I do best," she argued.

When Cavan started up the three steps, Baynes said, "There'll be no trouble." Cavan backed off.

Baynes was in his sixties, a scrawny geezer who nonetheless projected a degree of intimidation. He wore striped britches held up by suspenders over a white shirt, and no hat; the fringe of hair surrounding his pate stuck out in an unruly manner, and his thin nose, chin, and ears all protruded. He reminded Holt of a bantam chicken.

Baynes patted the chair at his right hand and said to Sam, "Please sit." She thanked him and did.

"I own a library of three thousand volumes." Baynes's tone was avuncular; at the same time Holt wondered what that had to do with anything, he half expected him to touch Sam's knee. "Do you know Balzac?"

"Not personally."

Baynes smiled politely. "I'm forgetting my manners." He gestured with his glass. "Would either of you care for a cold drink? I'm having lemonade with a touch of gin."

Lerner's beverage of choice, Holt thought, and so much for Biblical cautions against strong drink. He crossed his arms on the porch rail, feeling like the odd man out at this soiree.

"Plain lemonade would be nice," Sam said. Baynes glanced at Holt and he shook his head, mostly out of perverseness.

"What has brought you to my home?" Baynes asked.

Cavan and his men watched with the anticipatory relish of men placing bets on a bear-and-bull fight. "We hope to negotiate a peace between you and the people of Golem," Sam said.

"There will be peace," Baynes said, talking to her but staring at Holt, "when Reich accepts my fair offer."

"Reich does not wish to sell," Sam said.

Baynes smiled. "But he does."

Sam set her glass of lemonade on the porch deck. "This is a nation of laws."

"There are laws and there are laws." Baynes made a signal with his hand, as if to demonstrate his point.

Instantly four women filed from the front door and formed a semicircle behind Baynes's rocking chair. One lay a hand on Baynes's shoulder, and he stroked at it in an absent manner.

All of the women were pretty and none could have been older than twenty-five, and each wore a long-skirted gown. "My wives," Baynes said.

The four kept their eyes lowered. Baynes raised his empty glass; one woman took it and the four retreated in single file. The last, a tall chesty woman with blond hair encased in a snood dropped her handkerchief. She took her time retrieving it while the others went on. When the blond followed, she paused in the doorway and gave Holt a frank, steady look that she held for a good five seconds before entering the house.

"Are you behind the cattle mutilations?" Sam said. When Baynes did not answer, she pressed, "Do you employ a very tall man with distorted features?"

"No." Baynes smiled pleasantly. "Prove me a liar."

One of the wives—not the blonde—returned with a fresh lemonade for Baynes. Holt could smell the sloey scent of the gin. "You're a hired gun, then, you and your gentleman friend," Baynes said. "And you plan to take the law into your own hands."

"You already have," Sam accused.

Baynes had been holding his wife by the wrist, and now he set down his glass and stood. The woman's expression was neutral except for her eyes, which flashed with fear. She turned her back to them without a word from Baynes. He said to Sam, "Allow me to show you something."

Cavan and his boys looked pleasured; for his part, Holt felt vaguely nauseous.

The brunette's gown buttoned up the back. Baynes undid the buttons from the collar to the base of the woman's rib cage, so the woman had to cross her arms over her breasts to keep the dress from falling away. All of this struck Holt as sickly obscene.

Baynes parted the material. The woman's back was crisscrossed with fresh red welts.

"Here is what I wish." Baynes still spoke to Holt. "You will leave my spread and, once you have gathered your belongings, leave Golem and this territory. If you do not, I will have the two of you brought to me."

The brunette's head was bowed and she was shaking. Baynes indicated her scarred back. "First," he went on, "your woman will be stripped to the waist and horsewhipped by me while you watch. Second, my men will crush both of your hands so they'll never mend right. You'll not wield a weapon again, Mr. Gunman, and be for the rest of your days at the mercy of every mother's son."

Baynes slapped the brunette's rump with the back of his hand, not hard, but she moaned softly anyway before retreating into the house.

"Do you believe me?" Baynes said.

"What I believe," Holt said to Sam, "is it's time we moseyed on out of this freak show."

It was noon when they rode past Cavan and his thugs and out through the gate, the day no brighter than it had dawned. A gusty wind came up, and Holt buttoned up his vest and jammed his Stetson down tighter. "You okay?" he asked Sam.

"You mean did he scare me?"

"Actually, I meant are you cold?"

She was wearing a pair of black leather britches in which Holt had not previously seen her, a hat like his but buff-colored, and a cotton blouse under a serge jacket. "I'm not cold," she said.

"So," Holt said, "did he scare you?"

"Yup," Sam said without hesitating. "What he threatened—he could do it."

"I won't let him."

"My savior." She tried to make a joke of it, but Holt could see that the tail end of their interview with Baynes had shaken her up.

They moved on under the dark-clouded sky toward the low mountains. Holt's stomach growled, but it would be the better part of three hours before they reached Golem. Beyond the mountains lightning flashed, and five seconds later the boom of thunder reached them. "We could run out," Holt said.

"What about Reich?"

"We'll leave after dark."

Sam considered. "I guess we won't."

"Why not?"

At first Sam's answer seemed unresponsive. "When I was working in the magazine's main office in Boston, they sent me to a spa in the Berkshires. I was supposed to write a travel piece about one of the resorts. It was exclusive, isolated, and as it turned out, not what it seemed. My first night, in the cocktail lounge, a very drunk man stuffed a hundred-dollar bill down the front of my dress and asked if I did 'special stuff.' "

"Did you?"

"Very funny. It turned out this spa maintained a house with a dozen women where proper Boston Brahmins could get services their wives didn't likely offer."

Holt wanted a smoke, but not badly enough to rein up to build one. He'd always had a secret admiration for men who could roll a cigarette on a moving horse; he generally ending up spilling tobacco all over himself.

"I learned that the women had been brought over, mostly from Ireland," Sam said. "They'd been promised jobs as chambermaids and waitresses, and instead found themselves sold into white slavery, and no one to turn to. The slaver was a man named Montgomery, and when I confronted him, he threatened me, and I mean seriously. He scared me as much as Baynes."

They started up the slope toward the mountain pass.

"I thought about forgetting the whole business," Sam went on, "and then I thought, 'I'm a reporter, goddamn it.' I wrote the story, and when they arrested him, I covered the trial. After he was convicted and sentenced, he jerked loose from the deputies, charged at me, and managed to blacken my eye before they got him wrestled to the floor."

"Jesus," Holt said.

"Yeah," Sam said. "I wasn't too pleased." She reined up and turned in the saddle to face him. "It cost me a lot in pancake makeup, but I hadn't backed down, and I'd done the right thing."

Holt got it now. "This is a different deal."

"No it's not," Sam insisted. "And that's the first reason we're not going to run out: It wouldn't be right. Baynes is a son of a bitch who needs someone to rub his nose in the dirt."

The clouds reluctantly released a few drops of rain. "Doesn't have to be us," Holt said.

"Who else? Reich? Lerner?" Sam hunched her shoulders,

but the rain backed off. "You saw what Baynes did to that woman."

"That's eating at you."

"He's a pig," Sam spat. "He ought to be down in the mire with the rest of the swine."

Sam booted the bay in the flanks somewhat harder than necessary and rode on up the trail. Holt followed, framing his response with care. Finally he said to her back, "Revenge is always a poor motive."

She waited for him to catch up. "There's a practical reason, too," she said. "If we run, where do we run to?"

Holt considered. "Mexico?" he suggested.

Sam gave him an angry look. "Are you deliberately playing at being dense?" she asked.

"What kind of a remark is that?" Holt's own dander was rising.

"Sorry," Sam said. "Look, Holt, I like riding with you, but I don't plan to make a career of it."

That reminded Holt of his earlier thoughts and brought back his discomfiture. "I guess you and me come from different sides of the track."

"That's not my point," Sam said curtly. "We need the Big Man to clear ourselves, and he's here now."

"At least he was here last night."

"And he'll stay here," Sam pressed, "until Reich can convince Golem to sell out, or until we can get him and drag him up to Colorado to testify to your innocence."

Right about now, with Holt's mood matching the gloomy skies, that seemed like a faint possibility. Still, he couldn't argue with her reasoning, and truth to tell, he shared her aversion to being scared off. Holt held up his hand and flexed the fingers. "Still, I wouldn't much like Barnes's boys taking a sledgehammer to my mitts."

"I won't let him," Sam said.

"My savior," Holt said, going along with the gag. And then: "What the hell?"

Sam watched mystified as Holt drew his revolver, but then she too heard hooves on gravel, around the last curve on the way to the pass. "If you're about to say, 'Stay here,' don't bother."

Holt dismounted and handed her the bay's reins. "Stay here." He moved up the trail.

His back to the upslope, Holt rounded the curve. He saw a horse's fetlocks and then boots in stirrups. He moved another step and that gave him a glimpse of the single rider at the apex of the pass.

Elder Baynes's busty blond wife showed him an uncertain smile.

Holt's first thought was ambush, but the rounded mountainsides were bare of any cover beyond weeds, and as he advanced, the woman said, "I'm alone, if you're wondering."

Holt decided to believe her. He turned, meaning to holler to Sam to come ahead, but of course she was right behind him. Holt took back his horse and mounted up, rode the last few yards to where the woman was waiting.

"I'm Sarah." She studied Holt with deep blue eyes. "I suppose my last name is Baynes."

She had changed into riding britches, boots, and buttoned-up fleece-collared suede jacket. The snood was gone, freeing her blond hair to descend in a wavy cascade from beneath a cloth bonnet. She had high cheekbones and full lips, and was even more beautiful close up.

"I could be in trouble if I return," she said, glancing at Sam and then back to Holt. "Baynes is napping now and won't waken until suppertime, but they might talk."

"Who?" Holt kept looking around; he wasn't yet ready to accept that this wasn't some kind of trap.

"Zipporah, Naomi, and Rachel," Sarah said. "The wives. We get along well enough, and they've got their secrets, too, but if Baynes misses me, he will force them."

Holt remembered that he wanted a cigarette. He got out his makings.

"Leave him." Sam's tone made Holt look at her; it mixed sympathy and irritation, and he wondered if the latter had to do with the way Sarah Baynes was regarding him. Could be that he was misreacting, but for all the world it appeared that her look suggested some sort of future together.

Sarah gestured at the cigarette that was forming in Holt's hand. "Could I have one of those?"

Holt lit the smoke and handed it over. "Anything else I can do for you?" If he liked her look, it touched a nerve.

Sarah took a deep drag. "Take me to Golem," she said, "and then from this country."

Holt gaped at her. To his side, Sam said, "How about me?" He turned and she touched two fingers to her lips. "Sorry," Holt said, and went to work on a cigarette for her.

"You saw how Baynes is." Sarah was appealing to Sam.

Sam forked the smoke that Holt lit and gave her. She looked balanced between sympathy and jealousy.

"I haven't slept in his bed more than three times," Sarah appealed to Sam. "He's an old man, and he doesn't need the comfort of women. He keeps us for other purposes." She drew breath. "Such as what he did to Naomi."

"Has he beaten you as well?"

"Yes." Sarah said. "I live in constant fear."

"Why not take off on your own?" Holt blew out smoke.

"He would send after me. There is no guessing what he might do before turning me back." Sarah's blue eyes unfocused. "If you saw him, you would understand. He is ugly, grotesque, a monster, and Baynes might give him permission to ravage me."

Holt felt unmoored at this uncanny monologue. "Who're you talking about?"

"His name is Gutt," Sarah said, "and he is fiendish." She drilled her gaze at Holt. "You seek him. I can help."

Holt was not sure which of his needs she was trying to address—the apprehension of this giant Gutt, or his want of a woman for the last two years.

"Don't need help," Holt mumbled, and felt even more abashed when Sam snorted with clear disdain. "I already got a bellyload of problems with your husband," he said. "Stupidest thing I could do is run off with his wife."

"Don't flatter yourself," Sam snapped.

Holt finished making his own smoke and set fire to its tip. "I'm getting chilled," he said. "Already this day I've rode fifteen miles. My butt and back hurt, I haven't had lunch, Baynes threatened to break my hands, and it looks like rain." Holt flicked ash. "I hanker for food and shelter."

"He doesn't stay on Baynes's ranch," Sarah said. "But I know where he is."

Holt looked up at the sky as it released rain for true. Fat drops hit Holt's chin.

"You need me," Sarah said.

Sam's mood underwent another sea change. "You need to ride on down to your husband and your fellow concubines," she said.

Sarah gasped as if Sam had struck her.

"Hold up," Holt said, his voice low and gentle, the tone he might use on a lightning-spooked mare. "The sooner we see to this Gutt, the faster we can get ourselves loosed from several varieties of bad business."

Sam grunted and turned away. "Maybe we can make a deal," Holt said to Sarah.

"I will trade only for your promise," Sarah said, "that you will liberate me from that despicable old man."

"That can't happen," Holt said.

"Well then." She turned her back to them and walked her horse slowly down the hill, toward Baynes's sprawling spread.

Sam watched until she disappeared around the curve. "And what is it you want, Mr. Holt?" she asked pensively, as if abashed at her own vehemence.

"Two shots of bourbon and a beefsteak." Raindrops splashed off the brim of Holt's Stetson. Sarah Baynes disappeared behind the curve of the trail.

"That all?" Sam pressed.

Holt squinted his eye and proceeded over the part of the trail that disconcerted him most. "That and a little peace of mind," he said.

CHAPTER
TWELVE

The rain curtained Golem and made the afternoon dim as dusk. They'd donned oilcloth after the encounter with Sarah Baynes, but the ponchos offered only partial protection in weather this severe, and water drizzled through the neck hole and ran coldly down Holt's back as they rode down the street along the creek's left bank.

The town revealed no sign of life, which at first Holt attributed to the downpour. But then he noticed that the shops on both sides of the stream were shuttered and dark, except for the Pishon House; behind its bat-wing doors, the candles of the chandelier shined faintly.

"What's this?" Holt asked the wind. He reined up before the saloon and dismounted, Sam following suit.

As they entered the saloon, Robert Lerner rose from behind the bar, holding a bottle. "I never had a chance to search out where Shapiro hid the good stuff." Except for Lerner, the place was deserted.

"Who's Shapiro?" Holt shook water from his poncho and pulled it over his head.

"The tavern keeper." Lerner showed them a bottle of brown liquor with a fancy engraved label. "Single-malt scotch. A taste o' the heather, as they say." Lerner undid the seal and pulled the cork. "Join me?"

"Why not?" Holt advanced toward the bar, where Lerner was setting out three shot glasses. Holt got out his pouch.

Sam said, "Let me try. I've been observing."

Lerner filled the glasses to the brim, raised his with a steady hand, and said, "*L'chiam.* To life."

Holt tasted the scotch. It was okay, but it didn't have the smoky richness of his usual tipple, bourbon. Sam twisted the paper and licked it closed; the cigarette was a little bulgy in the middle, but Holt said, "Not bad for a first try," when she gave it to him.

Lerner tossed back his shot and refilled his glass. "Where is everyone?" Holt asked.

"Synagogue."

"Is it Saturday?" Sam asked.

Lerner shook his head. "Town meeting. People are worked up now that the mutilations have started up again."

"What are they figuring to do?"

"Let's drop by and find out," Lerner suggested. "I was fixing to go over, soon as I wet my whistle. For medicinal purposes only, of course."

Holt finished the scotch and pushed the glass toward Lerner. "First hit me one more time."

The rain had stopped when they left the saloon, although the dark clouds remained to threaten another downpour at any time. The creek beneath the footbridge was swollen but remained within its banks, though in this sort of desert country, a truly vicious storm could raise a stream five feet in thirty minutes. "You ever get flooded out?" he asked Lerner.

"Uh-uh. If it gets dicey, we open the ditch gates all the way and the water is diverted into the fields." Lerner smiled over his shoulder. "We think of everything. We're Jews."

Holt had been curious about the interior of the synagogue since first seeing the building. He found it little different from the Lutheran churches he'd known as a kid, though bigger and less rough-hewn, in keeping with the rest of the town. An aisle divided a dozen rows of pews without kneeling boards, facing a raised altar with two podiums and, behind them, an ark with double doors, which were open to reveal a large scroll. "The Torah," Sam explained.

"The first five books of the Bible, in Hebrew. It's read aloud at services."

To either side of where they stood at the back end of the aisle were staircases, and above was a balcony. The pews were mostly full, and as Holt was noticing that all the occupants were male, a man stepped to Sam's elbow and said, "You are welcome, of course. Women are seated upstairs."

Sam smiled at him nicely and said, "Not this woman."

Reich stood behind one of the podiums, apparently finishing a speech as they had entered, with, "What say you, then?"

The man beside Sam reached for her arm. "Don't," Holt cautioned in a low, hard voice. "It'll make her cranky."

Lerner laughed and said, "Come on." The last pew had a couple of empty seats, and Lerner led them that way.

A man stood near the front of the temple. "I say we mount a militia and take the fight to Baynes."

"Here here," Lerner said. Heads turned in their direction. Holt was about to slide onto the bench next to Sam when, from the altar, Reich boomed, "Come forward, sir."

Holt had not expected this and didn't much like it, but it was either do as Reich requested or flee. As he proceeded up the aisle, another man called out. "I fear for my family. What shall we do when they go from killing cattle to killing people?"

Angry murmurs followed Holt as he climbed the stairs at the altar's side. Reich gestured to the second podium. "Tell the congregation the results of your mission."

Holt placed his hands on the lectern and cleared his throat. Now he could see the women and small children in the sloping balcony, the kids fidgety, but the wives watching him intently, like everyone else in the assemblage. He searched out Sam's face in the back of the room. She smiled and nodded encouragement.

"Baynes denies involvement," Holt began.

"Louder, sir," Reich said.

Holt felt like a kid reprimanded by a schoolteacher. "I don't believe Baynes," he said, raising his voice, "but I also don't think you can prove him a liar, not so it will stand up in a court of law."

"We have no need of courts," a man called out. "I stand with action."

"You could end up in court just the same. Or worse."

It was Sam who had spoken, and every man's head turned to look at her, while the women in the balcony strained forward. Sam rose and came down the aisle to take her place beside Holt.

"This is Mormon territory," Sam said to the congregation. "We know that the hierachy in Salt Lake does not support Baynes's efforts to run you out, but if you push the issue, the council will be forced to take a side." She paused for effect. "Do you think it will be your side?"

Seconds of contemplative silence were broken by the man who had expressed fear for his family. "Of course not. We will be hounded out, and without the money Baynes has offered. Let's take it and move on. There is other country where we could settle."

"I like it here."

Again the heads turned, as Lerner stalked past the pews to join Holt and Sam. Reich frowned darkly at him. It was getting crowded at the podium; Holt eased back to stand beside the ark.

"We made this place," Lerner exhorted the crowd. "We turned barren dirt into a garden. Why should we let ourselves be driven out? By what right does this man Baynes presume to encroach upon us?"

Holt was impressed. Whatever Lerner's weaknesses, this oration was surely not informed by the influence of Single-malt Scotch.

"Have you naysayers forgotten the Torah?" Lerner went on. "Is Baynes our pharoah, to send us into exodus?"

Angry mutterings issued from the assembly. Reich gave Lerner a dark look. Someone shouted, "We have the strength of numbers. I say we use our strength." Others called out support, and one voice rose above the din to cry, "Let us avenge ourselves."

Holt didn't like Lerner's rhetoric any more than Reich, but for different reasons. He moved back to the podium and placed his hand on Lerner's arm.

"My partner is right," Holt said to the crowd before Lerner could cut in. "If you attack Baynes, you are fated to lose."

"This man speaks truly," Reich said.

"Another thing," Holt went on. "No one has died yet." He leaned forward, his hands gripping the podium's edge. "Who among you is willing to start the killing?"

The congregation set stock-still and quiet. The silence was broken by Lerner. "I am." His tone was soft, but it reached every corner of the room.

Holt was alarmed. He truly believed that an assault on Baynes would one way or the other sound the death knell for Golem and its citizens. Before he could marshal his thoughts, Lerner said, "But killing may not be necessary."

Lerner paused for effect. Reich said, "Your liquor speaks for you."

Lerner ignored him. "I propose that we do raise a posse," he said, "but not to attack Baynes directly. We merely take back in kind the cattle he has murdered. An eye for an eye."

"Exodus twenty-one," Holt murmured. He raised his voice to the congregation. "It will escalate the conflict."

"Show me a better idea, Mr. Holt," Lerner interrupted. "What good have you done so far?"

Holt was taken aback.

Lerner smiled sinisterly and said to the group, "Who will ride with me?"

Reich said, "Stop this. It will not conquer the golem."

Lerner gave him a cool look. "There is no golem. He is a man, and you know it—you and Baynes."

"What is that supposed to mean?" Once more Reich and Lerner had the congregation's attention.

"That's for you to explain," Lerner said in a pitch too low for the people in the pews to hear. Reich's face purpled, but before he could respond, Lerner called out, "I ask again: Who will join me?"

Men began to rise, amid a hubbub that had now spread to the women in the balcony. The aisle was jammed with people streaming toward the altar.

"Nice work," Holt said in Lerner's ear. Holt was furious.

"I didn't do badly, did I?" Lerner smiled.

It was all Holt could do to forfend from strangling the man. "You did plenty," Holt snarled.

Lerner moved to the edge of the altar to shake the hands of his supporters. He muttered something encouraging to one of them, then glanced over his shoulder at Holt. "Soon as I finish up here," Lerner murmured, "what say we get back into that scotch?"

Holt and Sam retired to the saloon under a renewed drizzle, and inside, Holt ordered two shots. Shapiro, the barkeep, was back on the job, and shook his head when Holt produced his pocketbook. "Tin roof."

"What's a tin roof?" Holt demanded.

"It's on the house," Shapiro said. "Bartender joke."

Holt snorted and brought the drinks to the table where Sam waited. "We ought to eat," she said as he sat down.

"I hate to ruin a good drunk with food."

"Are we drowning our sorrows?" Sam said archly.

Holt downed the shot. "Just taking them out for a little swim." He returned to the bar for a refill.

By the time he got back to the table, Lerner had joined Sam. "What gives?" Holt said abruptly. "Roping me into this was your idea originally."

"I was pressing Reich's hand." Lerner helped himself to Holt's drink. "Would you mind making me a smoke?"

Holt drew a breath, reached across the table to grab Lerner by the lapels and jerk him down so his nose came within an inch of colliding with the table's planks. He held him like that until someone cleared their throat behind his shoulder.

Holt let Lerner go and looked up to see the waitress from the restaurant. She balanced a tray on one hand, from which she dealt out dishes.

"They deliver, and I took the liberty of ordering for us." Lerner adjusted his twisted collar.

When the waitress removed the tin cover to reveal a beefsteak and potato pancakes, with young carrots and thick slabs of bread, Holt abandoned his mad in favor of hunger. He addressed himself to the steak, and Lerner had the prudence to keep silent until Holt was mopping the last of the meat juice.

"I'm doing what I believe is right," Lerner said then.

Holt set his fork aside. "You are playing games. What I can't reckon is why."

"For the commonweal," Lerner averred.

"You really mean to provoke a war?"

"You can stop me." Lerner drank from a schooner of beer. "By stopping Gutt."

"I might do that." Holt noted the glare of Sam's gaze and knew she was thinking of Sarah Baynes, and to hell with her. Holt felt good. He stood abruptly and went to the bar. "I'll have some of that fancy scotch," he said to Shapiro.

"The good stuff'll cost you."

"Nothing in life is free."

Shapiro produced the ornately labeled bottle, noted the level had gone down. "Me and Lerner got to have a talk," the bartender said. "Fifty cents."

Holt tossed two ones on the bar. "Make it a triple," he said. "The change is for you."

"Appreciate it." Shapiro left the bottle and placed a water tumbler beside it.

Holt felt slow-witted and irritated at the same time, and when Sam appeared at his side and said, "So now what?"

Holt replied, "So now I think I'll get watered." He half filled the glass.

Sam gave him a long sad gaze that brought on a momentary flash of depression. "Me, I think I'll turn in early."

"Good idea." Holt's voice had thickened.

"Yes it is." For her part, Sam sounded bright as a bird. "Good luck." She turned toward the table where Lerner sat.

"You fancy him?" Holt said.

Sam sat down across from Lerner. Without looking back, she said, "Go to bed, Holt. You're starting to slur."

Holt felt ineffably embarrassed, but he *was* drunk and full of that drunkard's notion of denial, so he finished what was left in the glass, taking his time drinking, and pointedly ignoring Sam.

When he turned toward the stairs—too late to make them without staggering, and no help for that—she was holding Lerner's hand across the table. Holt swallowed his anger and proceeded to the second floor, none too elegantly.

The room was sparsely furnished, with a sideboard containing a washbasin and piss pot, a double bed and nothing else. Holt was working at the buttons of his pants when someone said, "I've been waiting ever so long."

Holt grabbed at his gun, missing in the darkness, and decided the hell with it. He was too drunk to worry about being bushwhacked, but managed, "Who goes there?"

A match flared, and his eyes became accustomed to the more gentle light of a kerosene lantern.

It illuminated Sarah Baynes, lying naked upon the blankets. "I'd like to reopen our negotiations." She wriggled.

Some last sober part of Holt rose up and suggested, *No*.

Holt told it to shut up and skinned down his britches. He stubbed his toe on the bedpost and fell half atop her. "That's the way," Sarah said.

"Is it?" Holt got out.

Her arms were around him. "You judge," she murmured as her flesh pressed against his.

CHAPTER
THIRTEEN

Holt wakened to a glare of sunlight that matched the bright flashes of hangover pulsating in his brain. He was on his back and alone in the bed. The light brightened and Holt turned to see Sarah Baynes at the window parting the drapes. She was naked as he. "Hey," Holt yelped. "Get back from there."

"It's a pretty day to be alive," she said. "That storm front has moved off toward Kansas." She smiled. "No one can see in."

Holt sat up and moaned. He had plenty enough to moan about.

"How do you feel?" Sarah asked.

"Like someone dropped a sash weight on my head and crapped in my mouth," Holt said.

Sarah grinned sexily. "I know something that will make you feel better."

"Three cups of black coffee." Holt held up a hand. "Back off." In fact she looked extremely desirable, backlit by the sun's rays, her high firm breasts ... "There'll be none of that," Holt said, admonishing himself as much as her.

He felt gloomy and stupid, another dumb hombre who'd let himself be led around by his mule. "Get dressed," he ordered. She did, unselfconsciously, while she watched him wash and pull on his own things.

"Any chance of me getting you back before Baynes finds out you've run off?" Holt asked.

"No." She was enjoying herself. "I'm sure he's found the note by now."

"Note?" Holt yelped. He felt neck deep in the creek with the water rising. "What did it say?"

"That you forced me to go with you."

Holt tucked his shirt into his trousers. "Why'd you do a thing like that?"

"To make it happen." She finished buttoning her blouse.

A hand rapped on the door. To Holt it sounded like someone driving the final nail into his coffin.

Sarah crossed the room and opened the door.

Sam's expression started with astonishment and marched rapidly on to fury. She pushed past Sarah and stood arms akimbo before Holt. "What the hell is going on?"

His headache blossomed. "I spent the night with her," he said levelly.

"You plan to blame it on liquor?"

"Right you are," Holt said. "Regardless, it can't change what happened." He jutted his chin past her to indicate Sarah. "She thinks it'll make me take her with us when we go."

"We're going today, this morning," Sarah said. "You've got no choice about leaving, and no more reason not to take me."

"Don't tell me my choices," Sam snapped.

"He'll send men," Sarah insisted. "Cavan and his five boys, maybe even Gutt. You can't face up to all of them."

The bad news was coming in waves, and another glum notion hit Holt. "Lerner," he remembered. "He never gave me an answer. Did you talk him out of his posse notion?"

"No," Sam said.

"Oh Christ. Please don't tell me he rode after Baynes's cattle."

"He didn't, but . . ." She gave Sarah a significant look.

"I'm not a spy," she said.

"I got Lerner to hold off until tomorrow—at two in the morning," Sam said to Holt. Her anger seemed to be waning a bit. "A lot of the men at last night's meeting got cold feet, but he's got the backing of at least a few, and he'll be drilling them today." Sam hesitated. "I told him we'd go along."

"Oh great," Holt said.

"They're goners without us to lead them."

"*Us?* Who promoted you to lieutenant? One lesson with a gun and you're Calamity Jane."

"I shot a man," Sam said, almost lightly. "It wasn't that hard."

Sarah's expression had turned pale and uncertain. "You can't win. Even with a dozen men, you likely won't prevail over Cavan, and surely not over Gutt. We must go."

"You're not going anywhere with us," Sam told her. "Not now and not ever."

"If it's about your man—" Sarah said.

"He's not my man." Sam looked at him. "I guess we've established that." But to Holt's relief, her voice was calm and even a bit amused. "What now?" she asked.

"First I irrigate my brain with hot java," Holt said, "and then we get down to cases." He frowned at Sarah and let out a sigh. "You might as well come down with us," he said. "I reckon we've already progressed past the fire to the frying pan."

Sarah attracted her share of looks on the street. They were approaching the footbridge when Holt heard, from somewhere on the other side, the first volley of gunfire.

Holt drew his revolver and made for it. The shooting, which continued in bursts separated by pauses, was coming from behind the café. Holt flattened himself against the back end of the side wall, cocked the weapon and peered cautiously around.

It was not Cavan's crew after all, but three men firing from a spread-legged stance, under the direction of Robert Lerner. Holt holstered his gun and advanced toward them. Their guns were various as they, ranging from one's lever-action Winchester rifle to another's short-barreled .22, about as useful as a slingshot. The third carried an antique Kentucky flintlock; Holt hadn't seen one since he was a kid.

Lerner spotted him and told the men to reload and take a break. Sam and Sarah caught up to Holt as Lerner approached. Lerner leered at Sarah and said to Holt, "Shapiro told me you got lucky last night."

"Watch your mouth, Mr. Liveryman," Holt said.

"That's *Doctor* Liveryman to you, Holt." Lerner was having a swell time. He indicated the men. "You ready to lend a hand?"

"From the looks of them, it'll be uphill all the way."

"Exactly why I need you. Unless you want to doom them," Lerner added offhandedly.

"That will be your doing," Sam said.

Holt raised a hand. "Rein up." To Lerner he said, "The situation has changed."

Lerner's amusement did not abate as Holt explained the pickle in which Sarah Baynes had put him. "So now the shoe is on the other foot. You're coming to *me* for help."

"I don't cotton to you putting these men's lives on the line," Holt said. "Nor do I mean to myself."

"You got a plan?"

Yeah, get that coffee that seemed to be receding into the day's distance, Holt thought. Aloud he said, "I'm working on it."

In the end Holt did get his java, but finished only a half cup before Lerner interrupted his breakfast. His steak and scrambled eggs were still grilling when the liveryman arrived at the café. "We got visitors."

"How many?"

"Two. Cavan and another. Cavan's carrying a white flag."

Sam frowned. "What do you make of that?"

"Nothing until I talk to him." Holt pushed from the chair. "Have your boys keep a sharp eye in all directions. Could be others mean to sneak in."

Holt exited in time to see Cavan and his pard ride off the

bridge and turn their horses toward him. Cavan dismounted, keeping his hand well away from his gun. From fifty yards down the street, out of effective pistol range, he called, "I've come to palaver, Holt."

Holt wasn't yet ready to take him at his word, and felt a nagging edge of fear as he advanced to meet the man.

But Cavan kept his hands clear as they met in the middle of the street. "You seriously plan to mount an assault with them marksmen up on the rooftops?" Cavan spit into the dirt. "They don't look like they could hit their own ass with both hands."

"How'd you know?"

Cavan grinned. "Soon as we rode in, they're popping up to gawk at us," He shook his head. "You got a ways to go with them. I was observing for a time while they took their target practice. Spyglass."

"I don't see any spyglass," Holt said.

"My other boy has got it. Now he's observing us, so there's a witness in case any of your yahoos gets an itchy trigger finger and by some stretch is lucky enough to hit me instead of shooting himself in the foot."

Cavan pushed up the brim of his derby with his forefinger. Holt saw Sam on the boardwalk before the café, her hand resting casually on the butt of her gun.

Cavan nodded over his shoulder at the other man. "Thing is, if me or Buddy there don't get out of here alive, it's all over for you and this town. Salt Lake will have to send in the militia, your Jew pals will be run out, and Baynes won't have to spend a dime."

Cavan grinned on. "From that point of view, Baynes probably wouldn't mind if you shot me. But if I thought you would, I'd not have rode in."

"What do you want?"

"Two things originally, but now I got one more. That's to tell you that if you and your clown army set one foot on Baynes's territory, we'll cut you down like staked goats."

Cavan glanced at Sam. She was edging closer along the boardwalk, but Cavan seemed unconcerned. "Next is to remind you what Baynes said already: Skeedaddle on out of here or face the consequences."

Sarah stood at the café door beside Lerner. Cavan pointed at her. "Last is that of course you got to give back the woman."

"Baynes has already got too many women for one man."

"He don't want her for himself. She's spoiled goods now." Cavan's coarse features twisted into a sick leer. "Baynes is gonna give her to me and my boys."

"No." Sam spoke from Holt's right, her voice firm but not loud.

Holt was afraid she was going to act rashly, and made the mistake of looking at her.

Cavan's gun barrel jabbed into his belly. "You got your pick of two futures, Holt. You and your mouthy lady friend can ride out of here free as geese, or you can stick your nose into Baynes's business and I'll kill you, now or later. If you've got to think about it, you're either a chowderhead or a suicide."

Holt stared back for a long moment before saying to Sam, "Give him the woman."

"Have you lost your mind?" She stepped off the boardwalk.

"Do it," Holt insisted.

"When pigs fly," Sam spat.

Captivated by this byplay, Cavan eased the gun back from Holt's middle.

Holt grabbed Cavan's gun-hand wrist and jerked it away from his body while dancing to one side. Before Holt could clamp down on his other hand, Cavan fired, but the bullet plinked harmlessly into the dirt.

Another weapon went off and Holt stiffened. He got a glimpse of Sam, aiming up the street at Cavan's pard who was still horseback but with his hands up. Sam had fired over his head.

Holt wrenched hard and Cavan dropped his gun. Holt tried to knee him between the legs, but got his lopping stomach instead, to no particular effect. Holt followed with two hard jabs in the same spot, and this time was rewarded with a grunt of pain from Cavan.

With his free hand Cavan uppercut Holt in the jaw.

It hurt like hell and Holt would have gone down if Cavan had not grabbed him by the shoulders. Cavan arched his torso, and Holt barely managed to pull back before Cavan butted him in the brow. Holt's feint was enough to keep his skull from being cracked, but the force was still sufficient to knock him on his ass.

Cavan rode him down and gouged at Holt's eyes.

Holt fought back desperately, punching blindly and in rising panic, and somehow luck managed to get hold of Cavan's shoulder. His fist mashed solidly into the middle of Cavan's face, and the big man's nose shattered against Holt's knuckles.

Cavan rolled away and Holt clambered upon him. Cavan struggled, but the bloody wash spewing from his nose was draining down his throat and strangling him. Holt aimed his punches at that general area and kept them coming until Cavan stopped moving.

It took Holt a number of seconds to catch enough breath to gather strength to roll Cavan on his side, so he would not drown. Holt gained his feet, stepped back and pulled his gun on Cavan. Sam said, "You okay?" She went on covering Buddy.

"I'll live," Holt said.

Cavan snuffled and came to. Holt tossed his neckerchief down in front of Cavan's face, and Cavan sat up and pressed it to his nose. "You know what you just did?" Cavan said.

"On you it's an improvement," Holt said.

Cavan spat blood. "My nose's been broke before, and likely it'll be broke again. But yours won't, not ever." Cavan got to his feet. "Guess why."

"I won't live long enough, is what I figure comes next."

Cavan was trembling with fury. "You can bet your last dollar and give the odds to boot. Stay or go, I'll find you and kill you."

Cavan waved and his partner rode to them, leading Cavan's horse. Cavan threw the bloody handkerchief in Holt's face, mounted up, and trotted away without looking back.

Sam was at Holt's side. "Maybe we should give Gutt up for another time."

Holt shook his head. "Cavan will be waiting for us to run out. He'll cut us down, me for what I did, and you as a witness—if he doesn't decide to take his pleasure with you first."

Sam paled. "So what now?"

Holt picked up his hat and turned to the café. "Let's see if my eggs are ready."

CHAPTER
FOURTEEN

Holt impaled the last bite of steak on his fork and used it to mop up runny yoke. The eggs were sweet and fresh; in some corner of Golem that Holt had not yet visited, there must have been a henhouse.

Sarah Baynes placed her mug on the table and the young waitress refilled it. Sarah sighed with pleasure. "It's my first cup of coffee in four years."

"You gave it up?" Holt's mind was elsewhere.

"Baynes won't have it in the house. One of the vestiges of his pious beginnings."

Sam finished her breakfast, a bowl of porridge with toast. "Why did you marry him?"

Sarah added sugar to her coffee. "My father brokered stock in Salt Lake City. He'd contract with the meat packers in Chicago to deliver a certain number of head at a certain price, and in the fall, when the beeves were fat, he'd buy from the ranchers to fill his Chicago contract. The difference in price was his profit."

"Just what I need this morning," Holt mumbled. "A seminar in speculation."

"It wasn't that speculative," Sarah said. "My father was shrewd and he made a good profit every year—except the last." Sarah stirred her coffee thoughtfully. "It was the worst winter since Brigham Young brought the first Mormons into Salt Lake valley in 1847. Ranchers lost three-quarters of their herds to the snow and wind and cold. In all the territory, only this corner was spared."

"Which put Baynes in the catbird seat." Holt was becoming interested despite himself.

"Baynes drove three hundred head north that season, and demanded fifty dollars for cows that would normally fetch twenty and which my father had contracted to sell to Chicago for twenty-five. My father agreed to the price."

"That doesn't make sense." Sam calculated in her head. "He was locking in a seventy-five-hundred-dollar loss."

"Maybe he feared the men in Chicago more than Baynes," Sarah said. "Maybe he expected a miracle. He did not get one."

The focus of Sarah's gaze softened in recollection. "Baynes vowed to drive him into bankruptcy and take everything he owned—unless my father gave me over to him for a wife."

"Your daddy sold you like a cow?" Holt said.

"Baynes planned it all along. I'd seen him eyeing me." Sam shook her head. "That's contemptible."

"My father didn't see it that way. The family was broke, while Baynes was rich, and he could give me a good comfortable life."

"Why didn't you run off long ago?"

"I tried to from the start, in Salt Lake when my father told me of the arrangement he'd made. Baynes sent men to catch me, and I was trussed like a turkey and rode all this way under a tarp on a buckboard."

"You believed you had done something to deserve this," Sam said gently.

"At first. I was raised Mormon, and I thought I must have done something to displeasure God. I got over it pretty quickly, although Baynes did his best to abase all four of us."

Holt got a prickly feeling.

"When that buckboard trip ended, Baynes whipped me," Sarah said. "Before the first snows, I tried twice to escape, and I was whipped then as well. In an odd way, I could almost accept those beatings, in that from Baynes's point of view he was punishing infractions. It was the other beatings I could countenance no longer."

Holt read pained sympathy in Sam's eyes.

"Once a month one of us was whipped for no reason, in strict rotation so each suffered four times a year. These special whippings took place outside in the barnyard whether winter or summer, and the men were invited to watch."

Holt didn't know what to say so he shut up, but his silence rankled Sarah. "And you were actually going to do it," she said with contempt.

"Do what?"

"You were going to give me to that hired gunman."

"No he wasn't," Sam interjected. "He was only trying to distract Cavan's attention."

Holt stared at her. "You knew that?"

Sam laughed. "From the moment you opened your mouth. You'd decided long before that the moral action was to take Sarah with us."

I did? Holt thought. "I reckon it better be tonight," he said. "With luck and cloud cover, we might make it."

"We haven't finished what we came for," Sam protested.

"No, but the odds that we'll die first if we stay are getting better and better."

Sarah looked pleased at the prospect of getting away, and Holt supposed she had a right. She had enough troubles of her own without taking a hand in theirs.

Which, as Holt proceeded to outline, were substantial. "Ever since we rode in, it seems that every ten minutes we make a new enemy. Reich will turn us over in a heartbeat if he thinks we're lukewarm on bucking Baynes—and besides, Reich looks to be playing a double game. In the end, I bet he betrays us no matter how this comes out."

"That did occur to me," Sam agreed.

"Lerner's a similar threat, especially if we don't take his side."

"Have we decided that question yet?"

"Yeah, we have," Holt said. "Those men of his are no

match for Cavan's mob, and I won't be party to their suicides."

"Okay," Sam said. "That reduces the issue to the possibility of us going to jail."

"Not hardly," Holt contradicted. "Cavan may get over his mad for a time, but I'll wager his partner, 'Buddy will talk about how I bested him, and by and by Cavan will come gunning for me."

"You can take him."

"Thanks," Holt said heavily, "but I'd sooner not have to try. Then there's Baynes. He's got two reasons to see us in pain. Us interfering in his ambitions is one, and we're sitting here with the other."

"The irony is that at the moment, there doesn't seem to be any practical way we *can* interfere."

"Yet another reason to rattle hocks," Holt said.

"Leaving one reason not to," Sam said. "Gutt."

"No," Holt contradicted. "Right at this moment, Gutt stands as the fifth serious enemy, and an argument that we put this off until another day. He's got Baynes's backing and the protection of Cavan's boys. I'm going to frankly admit to cold feet about taking him on this go-around."

"What about the next time?" Sam said. "Will you be scared then as well?"

She was trying to raise his gall, but Holt had no trouble keeping it down. "Could be," he said. "But for now, look at the facts. How are we supposed to find him with all these folks roaming the hills looking to wax our butts?"

Sam stared at him for a long time, then shook her head. Holt was unclear on whether the gesture was in frustration at the situation or disgust at his fecklessness.

"You are wrong about Cavan," Sarah interjected.

Holt looked at her. "How so?"

"He doesn't back Gutt. He won't have anything to do with him, nor will his men. Gutt scares them." Sarah toyed with her empty coffee mug. "I told you I know where he hides himself."

"You did," Holt said, "and I figured it was a vat of hog-wash to tease me into doing what you wanted."

"You don't have to go near Baynes. Gutt is elsewhere."

"How'd you get to be such a ball of information?" Holt asked.

"Baynes sent me to Gutt, with money and food."

"See here," Holt snapped, "I may not be the smartest pilgrim God set on earth, but I won't fall for such a fable as that."

"None of the men would go because they feared him. They assumed Gutt was dull-wittedly brutal and might kill for sport. But Baynes knew that Gutt was neither retarded, insane, nor stupid. If he hurt one of his wives, Baynes would hurt him."

"But of the four of you, why send the most willful?"

"Because I'm the only one who rides a horse," Sarah said.

She had plenty of quick answers—maybe too many.

"I don't say I wasn't scared silly," she went on, "but I did it. He is impossibly ugly and he radiates violence, but he did not molest me. In an odd way, I ended up feeling sorry for him."

"But not so much that you won't give him to me."

"Lately I've been feeling most sorry for myself," Sarah said tartly. "I'll do what's necessary."

"This changes things," Sam pointed out. "If Sarah is telling the truth, and I believe she is, we've got our chance to accomplish what we've come for. We can still get out tonight." She smiled at Sarah. "All three of us."

In the depths of his subconscious, Holt held a fear-driven hesitation about actually confronting the Big Man, a despondent conviction that he'd never get Gutt to confess. He could, however, imagine his neck broken in Gutt's hands.

"You've got to do it sometime," Sam said. "We can't run forever."

Holt regarded her. "Is now when you say, 'I'm coming with you'?"

Sam looked away, and then the moment had passed with

the appearance of Robert Lerner. He sat down heavily. Holt smelled no liquor on him.

"You consider what I told you?" Lerner said.

"Yeah," Holt said. "But right now I got to be going."

"Where?"

Holt gave him an exasperated look.

"You won't ride with us tonight," Lerner said.

"Not a chance."

"It was worth the effort, I suppose." Lerner was talking mostly to himself. "But maybe I'm not the poker player I think I am."

"What's that supposed to mean?"

"I was bluffing," Lerner said. "I won't lead those men to their deaths. I thought the show—the target practice and all—would push your hand, but I've walked away a loser before and I'm willing to do it now." He straightened. "There's got to be a way to stop Baynes. He had no right."

"Gentle down," Holt said. "I'm not running out."

"But what's to be done?" Lerner asked. "Baynes holds all the aces."

Holt turned to Sam. "Let's get out of here."

"This time I think I will stay," she said slowly. "Like you said, I'm green when it comes to gun business."

Holt should have been relieved, but instead was angry. He felt he had been manipulated onto a limb and then left to wait for it to break. Lerner's abrupt change of mind also irked him. "Might be best if you both left Miss Baynes and me to our business," he said.

Sam looked pained but did as he suggested, drawing Lerner away with her.

"You ready to show me where to find Gutt?" Holt said to Sarah.

"Not in person." Sarah waved the waitress over and asked to borrow her pencil and a sheet from her order pad, then set to drawing a map. "Gutt may have aroused my pity, Holt, but he also frightened the knickers off me."

"So you're not going, either."

Sarah licked the tip of the pencil and went to work. "Not in a million years," she said.

CHAPTER FIFTEEN

Sam found the heifer lying beside the trail to Baynes's spread, a quarter mile outside the Golem fence line. The sight of the animal threatened to bring up her breakfast.

This time Gutt had botched the job. Maybe he'd been scared away; when Sam had ridden out, she found the gate ajar, though no other animals appeared to have wandered out. Even a cow was not dumb enough to leave fodder and water for the desert.

This one must have been driven mad by the inexpert incision in its belly. It was long enough to spill the animal's intestines but not to kill it outright; it was alive now, moaning at the scent of Sam's horse. The feeling was mutual; the roan snorted and rolled its eyes at the rank smell of entrails.

Sam dismounted, jerked the horse's head down, drew her revolver, and put a bullet between the cow's eyes. The cow jerked, stiffened, then lay still.

Some elusive aspect of the half-killed cow bothered her. Gutt had never failed to complete his mutilation before, and if he was accidentally discovered, it would likely be the discoverer, not he, who'd flee.

She put aside her pondering to address more immediate concerns. She had teetered on the edge of sharing her plan with Holt, but she was sure Holt would object, just as she was sure it would work.

Assuming Baynes listened to her, she thought with a chill. But she had to take the chance, for the sake of her, Holt, and all of Golem.

She crested the pass that marked the boundary of

Baynes's traditional range around midday, and felt exposed as she started down the slope. At its foot was the cover of some boulders and a copse of trees near the spring pond that was the headwaters of Baynes's creek.

Sure enough, a mile farther on as she reached the flatland, Cavan rode out of the grove. He wasn't holding a gun, but his right hand hung by his side. His lieutenant, the one called Buddy, appeared next to him.

Cavan rubbed at his potbelly. "I can't begin to guess what you're doing here." He turned. "Can you guess what she's doing here, Buddy?"

"Maybe she's addled."

"Are you addled?" Cavan asked Sam.

"I've come to parley with Cavan."

"Imagine that," Cavan said to Buddy.

Sam hadn't gotten a good look at Buddy during the confrontation in front of the café. Now she saw a slight man with thin arms and delicate hands. He wore work boots, denims, and a vest. His head was too large for his body, and his face was moony, with full lips slackly parted and small pupils that looked in different directions. In other circumstances that would have struck Sam as funny: a cross-eyed gunman.

"What you did," Buddy said to her.

"That was yesterday," Cavan reminded him.

"It was?" Buddy appeared momentarily derailed from his train of thought, and it seemed an effort for him to get back on track. "You drawing down on me," he continued to Sam. "It made me look dumb."

Cavan rolled his eyes at Sam, as if they were sharing a joke.

"Well, you see," Sam said to Buddy, "I was afraid if I didn't, you might shoot someone."

Buddy digested her remark. "I guess I might've," he conceded. "I can see your point."

Sam searched her memory and found the term: Mongoloid. The moon face was the tip-off.

"Cavan seen fit to tell the boys," Buddy went on. "They

started ragging on me and I got mad. There was gonna be a fight, but Cavan coldcocked me." Buddy removed his hat, a derby like Cavan's, to show Sam the lump at the top of his forehead, near the line of his thin close-cropped blond hair.

"That must have hurt," Sam said.

"Still does," Buddy said earnestly.

"But you ain't mad at me," Cavan said, as if reminding him of something already settled.

"I don't ever get mad at you," Buddy said.

Cavan laughed. "Which is why I keep him around," he told Sam. "That, and because he's the best marksman of all my boys. Hard to believe, isn't it?"

"How do you do it?" Sam inquired politely.

"I always see two. I'm seeing two of you now." Buddy was warming to the attention. "But I learned early on that the one on the left is the real one."

He pointed, and sure enough his finger was aimed spot-on at Sam's chest. "So the one on the left is the one I shoot. The one on the right ain't never shot back after that." Buddy laughed. "I made a joke."

The day had brought no clouds, and the sun was at its apex in the southern sky. Sam's brow was sweaty under her hat brim, but she forestalled from wiping at it. "Take me to Baynes. I've got something to say that he'll want to hear."

Cavan thought about it. "Probably not, but there might be sport for me and my pards."

Her sweat turned chill. "Then let's go," Sam said.

Cavan pointed at her hip. "Why don't you hand over that six-shooter first." He smiled his ugly smile. "I'd hate for you to embarrass me like you did Buddy."

They found Baynes on the porch as before, standing in an attitude of expectation. Sam assumed one of Cavan's men had been observing them on the way in and alerted Baynes. When they reached the house, she expected him to demand to know her business. Instead he invited her to dismount, his thin lips parted in a smile.

"This sun will wrinkle your skin prematurely." Baynes looked down at her. "You've seen my wives. Their skin is perfection, and Sarah's the smoothest of all."

Sam had nothing to say to that.

"We will go inside," Baynes continued.

Cavan followed her up on the porch. Without looking at him, Baynes said, "You know the times I need you."

Cavan went back down the steps, but Baynes's odd locution bothered Sam; it sounded like some kind of code. Baynes entered the house and she followed.

A long corridor ended in a wide flight of stairs. The walls of the hallway were covered in velour and hung with portraits, mostly oil paintings of men resembling Baynes. Where two archways opened on either side of the corridor, Baynes turned into the left one. Through the opposite arch, Sam caught sight of Baynes's three remaining wives. The brunette whom Baynes had exposed dropped her eyes.

Baynes said, "Would you care for something?"

This room was a parlor, carpeted with an ornately hand-woven rug on which sat a velvet-upholstered sofa and three matching armchairs flanked with side tables. The back wall was dominated by a large stone fireplace with a statue of the angel Moroni at the center of its mantel. Beside the fireplace was a connecting door. The two outer walls were broken by mullioned bay windows whose sills were inset benches scattered with throw pillows. The windows offered a panoramic view of Baynes's stables, barnyard, irrigated fields, and the mountains beyond. "It pleasures me to keep an eye on my operation," Baynes said to her back. "Please, sit."

She turned to see him waving her to one of the chairs. He stood at a sideboard holding crystal glasses and decanters of liquors. "I'm having gin and lemonade," Baynes said.

"Water would be fine, thanks." She found his manner jarring. Whatever she'd expected, it was not bonhomie.

She took an armchair while Baynes poured water from a pitcher and made his cocktail. He handed her the glass and stood over her. "If you are comfortable, it is time to speak your piece."

The fourth wall of the parlor was mostly bookshelves, floor to ceiling, and among the volumes were issues of *Harper's Illustrated Weekly*. Sam set her glass on a doily and rose to fetch a recent copy, found the page she wanted. It was a story of hers on the Denver Opera House, of no consequence in itself, but featuring a clearly recognizable line drawing of her beside the byline.

Baynes nodded when she showed it to him. "I thought I recognized you," he said blandly.

"As a journalist, Elder Baynes," Sam said, "I wield a certain power. I could write about what is going on between you and the people of Golem." She took a breath and played her ace. "It might not necessarily be flattering."

He should have blustered at this point about the laws regarding libel. All he did was drain his drink, sigh appreciatively, and fix another. When it was made, he looked at her. "That would be the ruin of me, wouldn't it." The idea did not nonplus him in the slightest.

Baynes tasted his fresh drink. "Might I ask something, Miss Lowell?" He did not wait for her response. "Do you believe that a man such as I does not anticipate and prepare for your nonsense?" Yet he was not angry, but amused, as if he knew a wonderfully comic secret.

"You *were* a journalist," Baynes said. "Presently you are a fugitive wanted by the federal government." He drank again. "Which, in case you were wondering, does have jurisdiction even in Utah, when it serves our purpose."

"Where did you get this idea about me?"

"One of Cavan's men has been in prison."

"Only one?"

Baynes's beak nose quivered with pleasure, as if she had just gotten off a bon mot. "This one was in the Arizona Territorial Penitentiary, and his term overlapped that of your partner by a month. As soon as you left after your first visit, he revealed to me that your Mr. Holt should be there still, serving a life sentence for murder."

"He's innocent," Sam said.

"I won't argue the point, since it doesn't concern me a whit. My interest is the price on his head, and on yours."

Sam worked hard to keep her voice on an even keel, but when she spoke, it cracked. "What do you plan to do?"

"I've already done quite a lot." Baynes stepped to the connecting door and rapped on it once. It opened and Cavan entered the parlor. "For starters," Baynes said to Sam, "I've made you my prisoner."

"To what end?"

"To demand your Holt's audience," Baynes said, "on pain of your death."

"It won't work."

"I'm sure it will, and I'll have you both." Baynes drank deeply and with pleasure. "See how this benefits me. First, it stops you and your man from interfering further in my business. Second, it enriches me by five thousand dollars."

The liquor did not cheer Baynes, but made him more adamant. "I've already dispatched one of my men for Golem, with word that if Holt does not turn himself in to me, you will be abused and then killed. The deadline is tomorrow morning."

"I mean nothing to him."

"Don't be absurd. He will come."

Sam had to hope Baynes was right.

"This was not the first of my men to ride," Baynes went on. "The moment I learned of Holt's identity, I sent one of Cavan's bunch to Saint George, where there is a Western Union telegraph station. There he learned that you are wanted as well, and he also sent a wire. Can you divine the recipient?"

"You tell me."

"A United States Marshal named Clennon Pert."

Sam rose, slowly and carefully. She feigned setting the glass down again, then whirled and flung it toward Cavan, charging Baynes in the same plunge. She got no closer than two steps before she heard the click of a gun hammer thumbed back.

"Watching you tussle with him could be fun," Cavan said, "but he's the hombre who pays me."

Sam paused, poised on the balls of her feet. Cavan had his gun on her and held the glass in his other hand, where he had plucked it from midair. "Quick-handed," Cavan said. "That's the term they use."

Perhaps Baynes had taken just the right dosage of gin to make him mellow, because he did not blow up. He clapped his hands once and the brunette wife appeared instantly in the archway. "You will be treated kindly for a time," Baynes said to Sam. "Until ten o'clock tomorrow, let us say."

Baynes signaled, and the brunette took Sam's elbow and led her toward the archway. To Sam's back, Baynes said, "Your fate lies in Holt's hands."

Sam worked to keep her shoulders from slumping. Isn't that just perfect, she thought.

CHAPTER
SIXTEEN

The elder surely did want to keep his distance from their hired monster, Holt thought as he rode out at one-thirty. Sarah Baynes's map put Gutt's hole-up as far east of Golem as Baynes's ranch was west.

He still felt irked at Sam abandoning him to take on this quest alone, even if it was for the best. He'd run into Lerner before leaving, and the liveryman told him Sam was up in her room, but when Holt rapped, he got no response. Maybe she was napping, or maybe she didn't want to see him at the moment. That rankled him all over again.

According to Sarah's map, Gutt's hole-up faced west, so he'd delayed his departure to put the sun at his back when he approached. He'd also felt the need for a rest; the fight with Cavan had reawakened the pain of his old gunshot wound. Now, though, he felt mostly fresh and the hangover had departed to bedevil someone else.

No track marked Holt's way out of town; the map used the creek as a marker line, so he followed it upstream. He passed the headgates of Golem's irrigation system and had been riding for another quarter hour when he saw a thin stream of smoke rising above the cottonwoods fifty yards ahead.

It might have been some innocent pilgrim riding from here to there, but early afternoon was an odd time to make camp. Holt dismounted and led the bay forward.

He eased his gun out when he reached a gap in the trees, revealing a little clearing in which the campfire had been built. A man was sitting before it on a saddle splayed on the ground, a big man—a very big man.

So the gun was trained on the man's back when Holt barked, "Raise the hands."

The man did.

"Stand up and turn around. Real careful, like you're walking on glass, which you are, you act up the least little bit."

Holt had never seen Gutt's face and was steeling for the shock of it, the ugly simian features, but when the man turned, he gasped anyway.

His trail clothes were ordinary enough up to the neck, but past there got bizarre. An oversized neckerchief covered the lower half of his face, hiding his nose and mouth and chin and even his shirt collar, and his eyes were invisible behind dark smoked glasses. Above he wore a sombrero with a hugely exaggerated brim, a ridiculous hat that some tourist might have bought in the depot's souvenir shop while the train stopped to take on coal.

But even a disguise like this would not hide the grotesque countenance of Gutt—and this was *not* Gutt.

"Doff the hat," Holt ordered, "and them glasses and hankie."

Beneath the cloth was a full beard. "What the damned hell?" Holt yelped.

He was looking at Reich.

Reich's eyes were abject with misery. "May I lower my hands?"

Holt remembered the gun and reholstered it. Reich dropped his arms and sat back on the saddle. A pair of bags lay beside it, but there was no horse in sight, and Holt's own mount had not nickered at another's scent. "Where's your mount?"

"It ran off last night, after I removed my tack."

"What are you doing here?"

"Repenting."

That was a big help at clearing things up. "Keep talking."

"I have sinned against my Lord and my congregation," Reich said. "You must take me back to face my just punishment."

"I've got other fish to fry," Holt snapped, but he was curious despite himself. "What did you do?"

"Another cow was attacked last night. I am responsible."

Holt could not have been more surprised if Reich had told him he'd decided to convert to Mormon. "*You* killed all those animals?"

"Only the one."

"Why?"

"Because I was frightened."

"Of this golem?" Holt scoffed. "I've told you once and I'll tell you now: He's a man."

"That was not what drove me. Man or not, I didn't believe Baynes nor any of them can be stopped, and I cherished life above loyalty. Now I see I was wrong on the first count, and I am condemned to Hades on the second."

Reich looked up. "But when I learned that Lerner never intended to attack Baynes with his little militia, I lost all hope, even though I myself had considered his plan lethal."

"How did you know Lerner was bullshitting?"

"He told me."

"I thought he was your enemy."

"He is, or was," Reich said.

"How about starting at the beginning."

Reich nodded sagely, as if that were a new idea. "Thinking that I must take a stand, I confronted him yesterday and told him that if he insisted on getting his men killed, I and God would hold him responsible for their poor souls. That is when he admitted he did not mean to carry through."

Reich toyed with the brim of his silly hat. "But Lerner had come up with an alternative that might succeed. He suggested we drive our hundred head of fat beeves to market immediately, as soon as we can make preparations. We have supplies and a wagon for them, and could leave as soon as tomorrow."

"It's a little early for market," Holt pointed out. "You'll have fresh grass and grain for at least another month."

"The animals are sufficiently sleek and meaty, and we are out of time."

"Looks like it," Holt conceded. "You agreed to Lerner's idea?"

Reich nodded. "You have seen that we make and grow all we need here. We could dedicate the profits on the beeves to stopping Baynes for good. We'd hire a lawyer to petition the Council of Twelve and the Territorial Legislature for protection, and if that was ineffectual, we'd engage our own ruffians to put Cavan and his mobsters on the run."

"Yeah, a range war is just what you need," Holt said. "What changed your mind?"

Reich studied the ground. "Soon after Lerner and I spoke, one of Baynes's cowhands arrived with a message. I doubt he knew the note's contents. Not all of Baynes's men side with Cavan or their boss, I suspect."

"Fine, but their moral stance doesn't concern nor aid us," Holt said. "What was on Baynes's mind?"

"He is tired of waiting. He stated that if within five days I did not persuade my congregation to sell, he would kill me."

"Don't Mormons make it a crime to threaten murder?"

"The note was unsigned," Reich said, "and written in a woman's hand, by one of his wives, no doubt. It would be struck down as evidence."

"So you panicked and went cow-killing."

Reich nodded unhappily. "I planned to kill one last night and two the next and so on, until the people accepted the hopelessness of the situation."

"How'd it go?" Holt asked sarcastically.

"Appallingly. I botched the killing and left the cow to die slowly and in agony. It was one of God's creatures." Reich looked ashamed. "Before I could put the beast out of its misery, I was frightened off by what turned out to be a deer."

Holt snorted.

"There is further treachery to confess," Reich continued. "In the letter I sent back to Baynes, I claimed credit for dissuading Lerner from attacking."

Holt felt a little sorry for him. "That's water under the bridge." Holt thought a moment. "How far is Salt Lake?"

"We need to go only as far as Provo, about one hundred miles north. It was connected by rail to Salt Lake last year."

Holt worked it out in his head. "With luck you could cover it in three days."

"If we leave before dawn, we may be able to get a head start on any pursuers Baynes sends."

"They'd still be able to catch up," Holt said. "Especially if someone tips him off," he added significantly.

Reich did not prickle. "I give you my word that I will face up to the man. If you like, you may keep me under surveillance, and I will go on the drive as wagon teamster." He smiled humorlessly. "As you can see, I am not very good on a horse."

Reich squared his shoulders. "But we have three men who are, and along with Lerner, they have been practicing with the cattle in the fields, in preparation for this drive."

"Four men is a skeleton crew for driving a hundred head a hundred miles."

"You and your woman would make six."

"Hold on a second."

Reich ignored him. "Then there is Mrs. Baynes, whom I understand rides well. You will be taking her with you, I assume."

"You're a little quick on the assuming," Holt said sharply.

Reich shook his head no. "You are a good man, and must redeem the poor woman."

"I thought I was a murderer," Holt pressed.

"I no longer believe that," Reich said, "and I will not turn you in."

"So long as I ramrod your cattle drive."

Reich shook his head again. "I pray that you do. I have

failed my people, but you have the power to redeem me. Yet even if you refuse me, you are free to leave unmolested. Lerner has given his word on this, too."

Holt believed him. "I'll think on it. Right now I've got four hours of riding ahead of me." Or two hours, he thought, if Gutt decides to dice me and have me for supper. "I should get back about nine or ten. You'll have my answer then."

Reich stared pensively toward Golem, visible as a green space on the desert vastness. "My advice," Holt said, "tell Lerner and the rest what you told me."

"They will be wroth."

"They'll get over it. You've done a hell of a lot for them, Rabbi, and everyone makes mistakes." Holt grinned. "If that doesn't work, tell them to turn the other cheek."

"I must face them as a man," Reich said.

"That's the idea," Holt encouraged heartily, thinking that the advice applied to himself as well. "I'd ride you back, but I'm running late and it can't be more than a mile's walk."

Reich kicked out what was left of his fire, tossed his saddlebags over one shoulder, and hoisted his tack behind the other. *"Vaya con Dios,"* Reich said.

"That Hebrew is a funny language." Holt laughed. *"Buena suerte* to you, too, Rabbi."

Golem's creek had its headwaters in a bright blue lake on a terrace three-quarters of the way up the next range of low mountains. A horseshoe of arête rose clifflike seventy-five feet above the lake's back end. From its rim Holt made out thick bunchgrass and leaf-heavy willows, an oasis of sorts. In the winter it would make a fine hunting spot, the deer congregating for water and shelter.

It was almost four in the afternoon, and although his timing was right, the weather had foiled his plan to use the sun, sending him to this position instead for reconnaissance. Dark storm heads were rolling in on a waxing wind that would bring them overhead within the half hour.

Below Holt the terrace garden was marred by the detritus of a one-time gold camp. Along one side of the creek were mounds of tailings, base metal and gravel into which not even desert scrub brush could sink a root. On the other side holding pools had been gouged out of the slope every few yards along a line fifty feet above the creek, and from each a deep, eroded gully depended.

These long-gone miners had used hydraulics in the most spine-wrenching way. Their method consisted of building a rock dam across the pool's mouth, toting bucket after bucket from the creek until the pool was full, and then blowing out the dam with a pick or a small charge of powder. The gravel that the resulting flash flood washed out of the hillside was shoveled into a Long Tom sluice box and worked with creek water—and then, if the miner's back had held up, he rebuilt the dam so he could go through the torturous process all over again. In a good day on a decent claim, a man might pick enough golden flakes from the Long Tom to make himself five dollars.

At least one of the long-gone prospectors had greater ambition. Up the slope at a point roughly perpendicular to the lake's outlet was a timbered shaft. It had appeared dark on Holt's arrival, but now, as the clouds came overhead to dim the day, Holt made out the faint glow of lantern light.

That he had found Gutt made him gloomy as the gathering weather, but at least when he made a cigarette his hands were steady. He smoked and stared into the wind. He was field-stripping the butt when Gutt came out of the mine shaft's adit.

Holt removed his hat and lay prone at the rim's edge. Gutt carried a pail in one hand and a gun in the other, and he paused before the mine to look around, turning in a full circle. Holt had a flash of the irrational notion that Gutt, like an animal, might actually sniff him out. But Gutt seemed oblivious as he proceeded down to the lake to dip his pail.

As he bent, Holt shouldered the rifle and sighted on Gutt's back.

The range was under two hundred yards, and Holt was confident he could hit Gutt where he wished. One slug in the leg would bring the Big Man down, and he would then show himself and the rifle and order him to throw his own weapon into the lake.

Holt aimed and squeezed on the trigger, but over the sights he saw all the ways this could go wrong.

He might get unlucky and hit an artery, and by killing his alibi, condemn himself—and Sam. Gutt, recognizing him, might realize he could not afford to take his life, refuse to follow his order, and wait with weapon at hand for his next move. Even if he did cripple the Big Man, Gutt might scramble up to the mine, where he likely had other weapons and would be impregnable. A horse had to be tethered inside as well, on which Gutt could flee.

On the tail end of all this pointless rationalization came the real reason why he could not fire: He'd been back-shot himself, and would not do the same to a fellow being.

Behind Holt, his bay whinnied with acute distress. As Holt rolled and rose he heard a chattering noise, and while he made his feet, the horse reared against its tether. Beneath its flaring hooves a rattlesnake was coiled in preparation to strike.

Holt dropped the Winchester, drew his handgun and fired. Half the snake's neck disappeared, and what was left flopped over like a hinge. The gelding tried to jerk free, but it was tied securely. Holt turned back to the cliff rim.

The bucket lay on its side by the lake. Holt scanned the terrace, found Gutt by the mine's mouth as the Big Man shot at him.

Holt grabbed up the rifle, fired too quickly and then again. When he took time to look, Gutt had disappeared.

"Jesus," Holt said aloud, thinking that only by God's grace had he managed not to kill the man.

The snake had stopped twitching by the time Holt sheathed the rifle and swung into the saddle. He had messed up this approach good and proper, and it was time for him to disappear as well.

His reasoning made sense, but like the rest of his plan, it didn't work out worth a damn.

An hour later and three miles downcreek, three points of stupidity struck Holt: First, he assumed Gutt would remain in the cave, believing himself pinned down. Second, he'd left Gutt in position to get a good head start. Third, he should have taken a circuitous route back to Golem.

All this came to him as Gutt emerged from a copse of cottonwood with his gun on Holt's middle.

"The hands." Gutt's voice was deep and guttural and appropriate to his size and disfigured shape.

Holt raised them palms out. His first good look at the man's face distressed him no little.

There were many ways a day could go bad; on this one, Holt thought, he was going to die. As if in confirmation, lightning flashed near enough so that the thunder followed in less than a second, and rain began to slash down.

Gutt sat a big black horse. Flecks of whisker spiked out of his dark jaw, and his eyes were nearly invisible at the bottoms of deep bony sockets. Even at this distance Holt had to look up to meet their gaze. Gutt wore denim coveralls and neither shirt nor hat. His hair was thick and shaggy and grew down to his shoulders; the rain pasted a coarse strand of it to his cheek.

"Your name is Holt," Gutt said. "That much they told me. I can guess what you want."

Gutt tossed back his head and lapped rainwater from his lips. Holt eased his hand toward his gun.

Without looking at him, Gutt fired. The bullet passed a foot to Holt's left, and he had to jerk hard on the reins to gentle the bay.

Gutt lowered his head. "Okay?"

Holt's shirt was growing sodden and he shivered. "Whatever you say."

Gutt studied him for a long moment. Despite his tone, Holt noted that the man's words were reasoned and thoughtful, but his next comment threw Holt off guard.

"Imagine being me," Gutt said.

"I—"

"No." Gutt held up a hand. "Listen."

His knuckles were gnarled and covered with thick, horned skin. "You may stare," Gutt said. "I have come to live with it."

He wiped rainwater from his face absently and his gaze softened in odd reverie and recollection. "My father was a preacher and a man of letters and a drunk. My mother died at my birth. Years later my father became crazed with the conviction that she was struck down by the Lord for bringing me into the world. He would have drowned me like a runt puppy if I had come from her womb a monster, but I did not."

Gutt stared away into the rain's sheet, as if it were a screen on which a magic lantern show of his life were being projected. "At the age when most boys reach full size, I went on. That's all the doctors know about this gigantism business: Something awry within makes you grow like corn in Kansas."

Gutt plucked at the bib of his soaked coveralls, but otherwise seemed oblivious to the rain. "When I was fourteen I began to change. To then my father had educated me well in subjects secular and churchly, though we never got along. His mood was tied with certain predictability to how much he drank. It was like the level of liquor in the bottle was a gauge, marked 'stern' at the top and 'violent' at the bottom. At age seven he broke my arm with his cane."

Gutt smiled oddly. "My life has always been ruled by omens and portents and curses that invariably are fulfilled. Are you an omen?"

It was the first notice he had taken of Holt in several minutes, but the question was rhetorical and Holt let it pass.

"I damned him when he fractured my arm," Gutt said. "I swore I would kill him 'when I was big enough.' " Gutt laughed. "Do you appreciate the irony?"

Holt nodded cautiously.

"When I was fifteen, I was as you see me now," Gutt said, "and from the liquor, my father was soft-brained." Gutt smiled once more. "Only a soft-brain would try to murder someone like me."

Gutt paused, and when Holt did not ask the obvious question, Gutt answered anyway. "I did only what he did to me—badly enough, however, so the surgeons had to saw his arm off at the bicep."

Holt stared at Gutt's hands, imagining what they could do to human anatomy.

"That was near the end of the war, in Springfield, Missouri." Memory now turned Gutt's smile sour. "I had to leave, of course. I went west, seeking fewer people and greater opportunity. But the portents and omens stuck to me like thistle burrs cling to lamb's wool."

Holt understood why Gutt was confiding all this to him: Gutt had the need of any human to talk, but rarely the opportunity.

"I could do the work of any two grown men," Gutt said. "But I soon learned that Destiny did not mean to admit me to the workaday world."

Holt reckoned he could see how that might be.

"On a farm near Grand Island, Nebraska, I hired on with a barn-building crew," Gutt said. "Three of the others made sport of me. Two left and one stayed."

Gutt wiped rain from his face. "In Virginia City, Nevada, I partnered with a man named Carmody. I had money and he had a claim, and we grubstaked together. The claim held silver, but he tried to play me for a fool. I am no fool. When I rode out, that shaft held more than silver."

Gutt's horse sidestepped and Gutt jerked the reins.

"North of Miles City, Montana," Gutt said, "a man called Jorgensen gave me a job bucking bales. He was the kindest Swede I ever met, but his wife was bored and liked to live dangerously. She flirted with me in mean ways." Gutt looked almost embarrassed. "When it came down to business, she didn't want it and I couldn't do it. Part of what's different about me, I suppose. It made me mad, and in the trying, she expired. They never found her, just like they never found the man in Grand Island, nor Carmody in the shaft."

Gutt stared at Holt. "What I'm saying is, those I do are done for good."

Right then, as if one cue, a white-tailed doe wandered out of the creekside thicket, its senses of smell and hearing dulled by the downpour.

Gutt turned in the saddle and shot the deer through the head. The animal flopped on its side in the mud and kicked its thin legs, while rain diluted the wash of blood and brain tissue flowing into the mud. Holt felt sick to his stomach.

"If you look as I do, you are believed to be a brute." Gutt's tone was casual, as if what he'd done was as natural as scratching at an itch. "Now and then you are called a brute. Eventually you become a brute." Gutt gestured at the deer as it stopped twitching and lay still. "Was that not a brutish act?"

Holt stared from Gutt to the slaughtered deer and back to Gutt. Rain splashed into his mouth, which he realized was agape. It was not so much the act itself, but the appearance of the deer at the precisely right moment for Gutt's purposes, a prop for his little play, as if Gutt truly was privileged with some eerily intimate relationship with nature and could engage it as his stage manager.

Gutt lapsed into silence for a time. "How do you expect women find me?" Before Holt could respond, he said, "Never mind. It makes me angry."

"So you killed Cat Lacey," Holt chanced.

"Of course I killed her, and I framed you for it." Gutt sounded impatient, as if Holt were missing his point. "I was paid for the deed."

"By whom?"

Gutt waved aside the question. "I will tell you I enjoyed it."

Gutt caught Holt's shocked reaction and looked frustrated. "But that's the point of my entire story," Gutt objected. "I came to understand that no cloud is without its

silver lining. There is money and pleasure in being a brute."
Gutt's eyes almost glowed in their deep sockets. "Do you
know what I feel most often?"

"No."

"I think you do. Say it."

Holt drew breath. "You feel sorry for yourself."

Gutt steadied the gun. "I'll kill you, too."

"I guess you will." Holt felt dizzy and frightened, and it
was all he could do to get the words out.

"You could have shot me." Gutt gestured at the Winchester sheathed beside Holt's saddle. "Why didn't you?"

"You know the answer."

Gutt was lost in thought for a moment. "It will not be,"
he said. "I killed the woman Lacey for money, but that is
something I won't admit and you can't prove."

"I'm not going back to prison for your crime."

"I could put you there." Gutt waggled the revolver, a
long-barreled .45 that looked like a popgun in his gnarled
mitt. "Right this moment, I've got the drop on three thousand dollars."

Gutt was enjoying Holt's chagrin. "I could truss you like
a turkey," he said. "Ride you out tonight to the nearest Federal Marshal's office. You'd yammer about how I was the
one they wanted, and when you wound down, it'd be the
word of me, a man who never has had a run-in with the law,
against you, a convicted murderer and escapee with no witness to prove your truth."

"How is it you've never been arrested?" Holt said, trying
to change the subject.

"I'm treacherous."

Then this strange conversation turned even stranger.
Gutt's eyes, framed by the hair rain-stuck to his face, once
more turned dreamy. "I'm also evil and sadistic," he went
on, talking to himself as much as to Holt. "I've got rage,
and I take it out on folk. On the trail I contemplate the
meanest ways to do it. Could be I'm a little crazy. I don't
know that it matters."

He came back to Holt, and seemed to have made a decision. "But I'm not that treacherous," he continued, his voice back to normal, "and I've done things that make me remorseful. Turning you in would be one."

Holt thought of Gutt's autobiography, and wondered if he rued maiming his own father.

"If you can stay out of prison, I'll neither hinder nor help," Gutt continued. "I have made up my mind."

Holt was reluctant to feel relief; this could be another bit of sadistic tergiversation.

"I have reason to fear you," Gutt said. "You can't kill me, but you could wound or ambush me, and even I can be tortured into confession. I feel pain like any man."

Gutt began to walk his horse forward one step at a time, spurring and reining. "Therefore," he said, "if you ever seek me again, I *will* kill you. Even if by some quirk you succeed in having me imprisoned, you will live every day of your life knowing it might be the one when I will return to you. You will be like a character in a Greek tragedy, the instrument of whose death the Fates have preordained."

The allusion startled Holt, at the same time Gutt's slow approach alarmed him.

"Do you believe me?" Gutt walked his horse another step.

"Yes."

"Do you know in your heart I can do it?"

"Yes."

"Will you leave me be?"

Holt sensed clear as daylight that if he lied, Gutt would know it—as Gutt knew he would get no answer to that last question. Gutt was beside him now, their horses flank to snout. Gutt's gun was within Holt's reach.

Holt wouldn't have tried it for a billion dollars.

Gutt reached up slowly and wrapped his fingers almost tenderly around Holt's neck. His skin against Holt's was scaly as a snake's.

Gutt leaned forward until his nose was six inches from Holt's. At that distance his face was nightmarish, the mask of an ogre that defied the order of God and Nature.

Gutt's fingers began to close around Holt's throat, the change in pressure subtle from a hand so gross. In time Holt could no longer breathe.

"A flip of my wrist," Gutt whispered in Holt's face, "and your neck bone will snap. Or I go on holding you like this, and it'll take three, four minutes. Near the end you'll kick and soil yourself, but my grip will never change." Gutt grinned horribly. "I've done this before."

Holt gagged from lack of air and the stink of Gutt's hot, fetid breath.

"I like this," Gutt crooned.

Gutt *had* been taking his mean fun after all. Holt knew he was going to die one way or the other, and had to make his move while he was able. He steeled himself.

A tiny second before he would have grabbed for the gun, Gutt released him and danced his horse back three or four steps.

Holt gasped in great lungsful of air. It tasted sweet as butterscotch to him at that moment.

"You'll remember that," Gutt snarled, "how my hand felt and my face looked, and how, just now, you were scared as you've ever been. I'll come to you in your dreams and your waking reveries, and each time, you'll know terror. Remember that terror when you entertain foolish thoughts of accosting me."

Holt *had* been terrified, and that made him angry, and he couldn't stop himself. "You been reading too many Greek tragedies," he snapped.

Of all the possible responses Holt might have expected, most of them lethal, Gutt chose to laugh. When it came to abrupt mood changes, Holt thought, Samantha Powell didn't have a patch on this hombre.

"I have done the job I was paid for," Gutt said, "and I am leaving this night. If I see you again, it will be in Hell."

Gutt holstered his gun. Just as well, Holt figured; both of them knew he was not about to try anything. But given the man's sudden jolliness, he decided to risk scratching one last issue that itched at him. "How did you disappear, that other night when I saw you?"

"You've reckoned that out already."

Holt was fairly sure he had. "You only struck when the grass was high. You hit the ground and slithered away, using it for cover."

Gutt smiled, the expression ugly as an old man's bottom. "I don't need high grass," he said. "Look away."

Holt did, wondering again if this was his day to die. But when he turned back thirty seconds later, he was alone in the wind and rain.

Holt pointed his horse toward Golem. His back tingled, in anticipation of that second bullet, which would, this time, find his spine and sever it as he had lately severed the rattlesnake's head.

But it never came, and sometime after nightfall, Holt reached Golem, soaked and shivering and recalling his interview with Gutt oddly and with lingering dread.

CHAPTER
SEVENTEEN

Neither Lerner nor Herschel was at the livery, so Holt had to see to the bay himself. He found a lantern on a hook and a tin box of matches on a cross beam above it. After it was lit and the wick adjusted, Holt removed the saddle and set it and the bridle astraddle a sawbuck to dry, then wiped down the animal as best he could. In the next stall was a musty-smelling blanket that he tossed over the bay's back; this night would be chill, and the rain held promise to keep falling.

The bucket was in the grain bin. Holt gave the gelding two pails, then raised the lantern glass and blew out the flame. He stood in the darkness another half minute, following the habit taught him by his father soon as he was old enough to help with barn chores. The first and only time Holt forgot, his father took his belt to his backside to remind him that a burning barn was no joke. Now in the livery, no spark pierced the darkness, and Holt went back out into the rain and toward the saloon.

A couple of old-timers were holding up one end of the bar, while behind it, Shapiro polished glasses with a white cloth. Herschel was swamping the stage. Only one table was occupied, accommodating Robert Lerner, Mordecai Reich, and three other men. Lerner was working on a shot and Reich a beer, but the others were not drinking.

Holt nodded as he went past, and Lerner said his name. Holt proceeded to the bar. He pointed at the ceiling and said to Shapiro, "Can a man get a hot bath up there?"

"Tub's at the end of the hall," Shapiro said.

Herschel abandoned his mop and hopped down from the stage. "Cost you six bits. They got water on boil at the café, but it'll take me a half-dozen trips to fetch enough to cover a big galoot like you."

Holt tossed him a silver dollar.

"I better keep the change," Herschel said. "It's raining."

Holt took off his hat and dumped water from the curled brim. "No kidding."

Herschel grinned. "When you going to teach me to shoot?"

"When you going to make my bath?"

Herschel darted into the back room for two buckets and a yoke, and went out through the bat-wing doors. Behind Holt, Lerner called his name again, but Holt was in no mood for Lerner's bullshit games. Shapiro said, "A shot while you're waiting?"

"Two," Holt said, "in a water tumbler. I'll take it upstairs while I strip off these clothes."

A hand gripped Holt's elbow. "Drink down here. We need to talk."

Herschel returned with the yoke over his shoulder and went upstairs.

"Some other time," Holt said. "I'm getting chilblains."

"This'll only take a second," Lerner urged.

Holt was too weary to argue. Shapiro delivered his drink, and Lerner not only paid for it but carried it to the table, like it was a carrot and Holt a donkey. Holt decided he was too weary to get angry, either.

As Holt sat, Mordecai Reich said, "I have confessed, as you suggested."

"And?"

Lerner answered for Reich. "We've got no time for recriminations."

Holt put two and two together and came up with the three other men, who were watching him carefully from under their straight-brimmed hats. He added in Lerner. "You and these men are the drovers," Holt guessed.

"Morris Levi, Ethan Cohen, and Noah Schwartz," Lerner introduced. "We set out in the morning."

"Hope the rain stops by then."

"Have you and your woman decided to help us?" Reich asked.

"I haven't asked her." That recalled to Holt his unanswered rap on her door before his bizarre odyssey to Gutt's hideout. "Where is she?"

"In her room, I suppose," Lerner said.

"You seen her since I left?"

"Now that you mention it," Lerner said, "I haven't."

Holt stood. Herschel had returned a second time and left to refill his buckets. The idea of a bath was growing increasingly seductive. Holt took his drink and excused himself.

By the time he got shed of his wet clothing, the tub was mostly full and steaming. Holt lowered himself into it with a prerolled cigarette and his drink near to hand, and was lolling with his eyes closed when the last two buckets of near-boiling water splashed atop what he was already immersed in.

Holt yelped and sat up too quickly. The cigarette fell from his lips and sizzled out in the soapy water. Above him, Herschel laughed. "I ought to pound your scrawny backside," Holt said, though in truth Herschel had been careful not to scald him.

Herschel backed off tauntingly. "First you'll have to chase me down the street. You racing through the rain buck-ass naked, that's something'd be worth a pounding."

"Nice language," Holt admonished. "You eat with that mouth?"

"Enjoy your bath, sir." Herschel gave him an exaggerated bow and exited.

Holt would have liked to luxuriate in the water, but it cooled too quickly, and beyond that, issues were nagging at him. Primarily he wished he'd checked on Sam. He rinsed himself, dressed, and went down the hall to her room.

He raised his hand to knock and stopped short. He went quickly down to the stairs, swearing under his breath.

He must have been more worn-out than he'd realized, tired enough anyway to have missed something significant. Sam's roan had not been in the livery.

Holt was halfway down the stairs when he realized the barroom was silent, and the five men—no, six now—at the table were staring at him. The newcomer wore trail clothes, was of nondescript medium build, and radiated no particular threat, although he did seem to have brought solemnity to the table. A dripping slicker was draped over the back of his chair.

"You'll want to hear this, Holt," Lerner said.

"There's plenty I want to hear." Holt continued down the stairs, went to the bar and asked Shapiro for another shot.

To his back Lerner said, "I wouldn't if I were you."

"You're not." But after Shapiro poured, Holt took the drink to the table and let the liquor sit. "Where the hell is Sam?"

The stranger delivered the bad news. His name, he said, was Horace Ramey, and he was sorry.

"Sorry for what?" Holt snapped.

"My first notion was to ride out. I've had a bellyfull of Elder Baynes."

"Get down to cases," Holt demanded.

"I wanted no part of this," Ramey said. "I was ten miles south when I saw I was doing the wrong thing. I couldn't have her on my conscience," Ramey said.

"You are being elliptical. Say your piece."

"Baynes has your woman."

Holt had guessed that, but hearing it aloud still rankled.

"This man delivered Baynes's prior message," Reich said.

"This man," Holt said ominously, "is going to be living in a world of hurt if I don't get his story damned fast."

Ramey paled. "She went to him and he kept her. The terms for her release is you present yourself. I wanted nothing to do with this turn of events, but you had to know."

"Now I do. Get out of my sight."

Ramey rose and made for the door. It was Lerner who said, "Wait a minute."

Holt glared at Lerner. "What gives?" Lerner sported his familiar smell of gin, and at the moment it nauseated Holt.

"You are forgetting yourself," Lerner said. "We've got to get her back."

"We?" Holt echoed.

"We'll discuss that," Lerner said. "Meanwhile, isn't there anything more you want to ask Mr. Ramey?"

Ramey reapproached the table tentatively.

"About Baynes's spread and where they are holding her?" Lerner prompted.

Events were piling one atop each other much faster than Holt preferred, so he worked to calm himself. "You've done the right thing, son," he said to Ramey.

"It could get me in hot water."

"I'm an expert on hot water," Holt said. "As to Baynes, what can you tell me about the lay of the land?"

CHAPTER
EIGHTEEN

Holt sat his horse within the cover of the copse of trees fifty yards from Baynes's gate, and asked himself what the hell he thought he was up to.

Baynes could read a man, and knew Holt would be coming. The yard, from the big house to the barn opposite, from the bunkhouse to the corral, was lit up like daylight by what must have been fifty lanterns. They hung from the porches, corral posts, and railings, and a line of them was strung on a rope bisecting the yard from the second floor of the house to the hayloft winch on the barn. Pegs had been nailed into the house's siding for more lanterns, so every approach was exposed.

Holt saw movement on the porch. One of Cavan's men stood and stretched, raising a shotgun over his head. Holt made out another, rocking on the back legs of a chair in front of the bunkhouse. It might have been Buddy. Holt guessed there was at least one more, patrolling the far side of the house.

The only way he was going to get there was directly up the road, with his hands up. At best that would mean jail for him, and for Sam as well if Baynes went back on his word. At worst, Cavan would be allowed to fulfill his oath to gun him down.

Holt tried to see some way he could turn around and leave her. He doubted even Baynes would kill Sam, and after she was jailed, he could maybe break her out, as she had done for him. But long before that, no telling what sort of ways Baynes would pleasure himself, or let his men . . .

Behind Holt a voice whispered, "Easy now."

Holt did not move except to tense the muscles in his legs while he raised his hands. He did it slow as syrup—and spun in the saddle, dropped the reins and slapped for his holster. His hand was around the gun butt and he could make out his target, ten yards away.

Holt started to draw and magic happened.

One moment the silhouetted arm of the other man hung away from his side. In an eye blink the arm was crooked and pointed at Holt and a gun was in the hand.

Holt let his own weapon drop back into its leather. Though the rain had stopped, the sky remained quilted with cloud. Holt could not make out the man's face until he was within touching distance.

"Feeling a little edgy tonight, are we?" Robert Lerner inquired.

The liveryman's tone grated like sand in stew. "About edgy enough to shove that gun where the sun don't shine, then pull the trigger," Holt growled. "How do you come to be sneaking up on a man?"

Lerner put the weapon away. "I didn't want you startled."

"Nice try."

"Also," Lerner said, "that was by way of demonstration. I lied."

"Several dozen times, by my count."

"Calm down."

"I don't want to." Holt heard the childishness in his own tone.

"Have a smoke," Lerner suggested. When Holt didn't reach for his makings, Lerner said, "Well, I'll have a smoke, if you don't mind."

Holt got out his pouch and went to work, using the rote of cigarette-building to calm himself, as if the tobacco and paper were prayer beads.

"The part about losing my wife over another woman was true," Lerner said. "The lie was about her being my secretary."

Lerner was talking about the abrupt termination of his doctoring career. Was it only two days ago that Holt had heard the story? It seemed like a lifetime.

"She was a prostitute," Lerner said, "and we fell in love. Her fancy man believed I was going to take her away, and he might have been right. Who knows how it would have turned out in another life?" Lerner came back to himself. "Anyway, he came after me and I outdrew him."

"You killed him?"

"Worse. He ended up paralyzed from the neck down, and he had friends. Prudence dictated travel."

Holt remembered the cigarette between his fingers. He lit it and passed it to Lerner. "Rein up. You learned the shootist's art in Newport, Rhode Island?"

Lerner blew smoke into the darkness. "In medical school," he amended.

"They teach the fast draw in college these days?"

"I joined a club," Lerner contradicted. "The Sons of the Pioneers, fellows interested in the romance of the West. We played at showdowns." He shrugged. "It turned out I had a natural aptitude."

"This is leading where, exactly?"

"To the fact that I can help you tonight. You don't have to give yourself up to Baynes." Lerner cleared his throat.

Holt heard hoove steps; in his preoccupation, he'd forgotten to wonder why Lerner was afoot.

Sarah Baynes rode into view, leading Lerner's horse. Lerner said, "I've got a plan."

Sarah leaned forward in the saddle and folded her arms over the horn while Lerner continued. Holt glanced at her now and again; she looked scared but determined, and he was not surprised that, after he rejected Lerner's proposal out of hand, she said, "I will perhaps be humiliated, but I can live with that idea better than the thought of you and Miss Lowell dead or in prison."

"If we do it by the numbers," Lerner added, "Sarah will hardly be part of the play."

Holt shook his head. "There's other ways."

"Name one," Lerner snapped.

He could not, of course, and while he was pondering his next feeble argument, Sarah rode forward, handed Lerner the reins of his horse, and then ducked down to run a caressing hand over the stubble on Holt's cheek.

"I know Baynes," she said softly. "I've studied him like a child's first primer. We will write this play, and he will be our actor."

She straightened, poised to spur her horse.

"Try to be on time," she said lightly. "I can't stand it when a man is late for a date."

The grass of the bottomland behind Baynes's house was still heavy with the rainfall, and Holt's front was soaked from collar to cuff. He hoped his watch wasn't getting ruined.

A shiver shook the irrelevant thought from his head. Holt was swallowing a sneeze when Lerner whispered in his ear, "We just got lucky."

Holt raised his head from the clinging grass of Baynes's third cutting to see the rider move toward them from the back of the house. As he'd guessed, Baynes had posted a man to that perimeter, but the lanterns here, pegged to the manor's wall, splashed light only a few yards from the building. The man rode out of their beam, dismounted and turned in their direction, reaching for the buttons of his trousers in preparation for doing his business.

"I've got delicate hands," Lerner whispered. "This is your turn."

Cavan's man was close enough so Holt could hear his stream splash on the grass.

Holt drew his Colt, held it by the barrel, gathered his legs under him and sprung. The man had three seconds to react, but his hands were full. Holt's weight crashed down on him, and Holt felt warm wetness on his thigh as he rode the man to the ground. Holt had to scuttle back to get a chance at his head, and even then missed the first time, giving the guard the time to grunt, too loudly for Holt's taste.

Holt struck at him a second time. The man cried out more loudly.

The noise was drowned out in Sarah Baynes's scream.

Holt clubbed the guard solidly in the temple and the man stopped struggling. Sarah screamed a second time. Holt scrambled back from the rim of the light.

Lerner was gone. Holt looked quickly around. Beside the corral, in which a dozen horses were dozing on their feet, was a haymow, and Holt made for it. A dinner bell chimed in with Sarah's third scream. Holt edged around the stack, searching for shadows.

He found the shelter of one that gave him a view of most of the yard, and still felt exposed. Baynes was the one working the dinner bell, on the porch, and chattering the striker around the triangle with vicious satisfaction. His other hand held Sarah's arm bent hard up behind her back. Pain and the garish lantern light distorted her pretty features.

Men exited the bunkhouse, rubbing sleep from eyes that turned from drowsy to bright when they spotted Sarah. Baynes marched her down the steps and turned toward Holt. On the other side of the haystack was a watering trough.

He bends us over it. Sarah's words on the pass echoed uncomfortably in Holt's mind. *If we are intractable, he ducks us until we believe we will never draw air again.*

"He took me, I tell you," Sarah sobbed under Baynes's grip. "Down in the mud like a dog, while others watched. It is they who deserve your fury."

Baynes slapped the back of her head. She stumbled. The elder jerked her arm up and she cried out more sharply.

Holt had to restrain himself from firing.

"Only now could I escape," Sarah sobbed. "I came as soon as possible, seeking your forgiveness and salvation."

Holt burrowed more deeply into the hay. The lanterns swaying in the breeze seemed to be searching him out.

Baynes reached the watering trough and skillfully worked Sarah's arm so she fell obediently to her knees, her face poised above the stagnant water. One of the men said something vulgar, and others murmured in agreement.

As Baynes bent over Sarah, his broad back was five steps from Holt. Holt stared at it, set himself.

"You are lying filth." Baynes's lips were close to Sarah's ear, yet his whisper carried in the heavy night silence. He reached around to the front of Sarah's throat, gathered a fistful of her shirt, and ripped hard. The cloth came away of a piece, and she was naked to the waist.

Cavan approached and handed Baynes a bullwhip. Baynes gazed around to prolong the moment. His glance passed over the shadow that hid Holt, and in his eyes Holt saw madness.

Baynes drove Sarah's head down into the water.

The men let out a collective sigh, and Baynes nodded his head, as if acknowledging a round of applause. It seemed to distract him from his purpose as well: He did not let Sarah up, and her legs began to twitch.

Holt cursed Robert Lerner for abandoning him and sprung from the hay. A speck caught in his eye, and he almost stumbled as his concentration was instinctively drawn to blinking it away. The hesitation gave Baynes time to react, rising and starting to turn.

But Holt was driven as much by outrage as purpose, and he managed to catch Baynes's wrist as the old man raised his hand in defense, releasing Sarah. Her head splashed from the water and she gasped. Holt stepped inside Baynes's free hand and dragged him around, got his arm in the same grip with which the elder had held Sarah.

Sarah crawled a few feet from the trough and vomited. Holt's muzzle was pressed hard into Baynes's temple. "Tell them," Holt said, his cheek pressed against Baynes's ear.

"Don't anyone move," Baynes ordered in a choked voice. The men froze; even Cavan, hand on his gun and staring at Holt, stayed still.

Sarah rose, brushed a strand of sodden hair from her cheek, stepped forward and drove her fist into Baynes's face. Baynes managed to turn his head so the blow missed his nose, but his teeth clamped involuntarily on his lower lip and a thin stream of blood appeared from the corner of his mouth.

A gun went off. Sarah stepped back from Baynes, breathing hard. The gun's report and the smell of burnt powder wafted on the breeze. Silence broke slowly, like the shell of an egg from which a chick was pecking its way out.

From the loft door in the second story of the barn where the hay was stowed, Cavan's man Buddy took a pace back, a pace forward, and tumbled from the opening to land face first with a sickening thud on the hard-packed dirt of the yard, his unused rifle cartwheeling once to settle out of reach. He had no use for it now: Blood bubbled from a hole in his forehead.

Lerner stepped into the light off to Holt's left, by the trough where Sarah had dropped to sit in the dirt. Lerner helped her to her feet with one hand, never looking away from Baynes's men, who had instinctively raised their hands. With his left hand Lerner began to undo the buttons of his shirt. Sarah stood and faced the gathered men, making no attempt to cover herself, challenging them to stare, as if to say it would not be she who would fulfill their puerile lusts, not this night.

One by one they looked away.

Holt heard soft footsteps on the porch. He edged back, the gun still hard against Baynes's head, until he could see the three other wives, accompanied by Sam. She seemed whole.

"Thought I better cover your action." Lerner gave Sarah his shirt and moved up to Holt's side, nodded toward Baynes. "We'll haul him along, I suppose."

Holt spoke in Baynes's ear. "The guns go in the horse trough."

Baynes's voice quavered as he gave the order.

The cowhands were unarmed. There was only Cavan and his remaining four men to watch. They filed forward, dumping sidearms and long guns into the water, except for Cavan, who hesitated a long beat.

Lerner cocked his revolver.

Defiantly, Cavan closed his hand around the butt of his own gun and held like that, daring Lerner to do something about it.

From the hip, without any aiming that Holt could see, Lerner fired. A tiny chip of the toe of Cavan's boot disappeared.

Cavan looked down in fair amazement. He was unhurt; indeed, the leather was scuffed but not breached. He frowned at Lerner, used two fingers to slowly pull his weapon. He stood over the water, let the gun dangle.

"What I told him." Cavan jutted his chin at Holt but spoke to Lerner. "It goes for you, too. You're both walking dead men."

"Not tonight," Lerner said.

Sam came down from the porch and Lerner stepped aside as she came up on Holt's flank. "Good to see you," she said. Sarah was on his right hand, Lerner's shirt buttoned up now.

"Let's get on with this," Baynes said.

Holt tapped the gun barrel against his temple, just hard enough to hurt. "Cavan," Holt ordered. "I want you and your boys in the middle of the yard, where we can see you all the way up to that pass. Any of you get missing, Baynes dies." To Lerner he said, "That work for you?"

"Fine. Even if they saddle up after we're out of sight, we can beat them back to Golem easy." Lerner thought for a moment. "One more edge." He sidled to the corral, dumped the gate logs to the ground, and moved inside. He picked out Sam's roan and ran a professionally gentle hand over its nose. "Have someone bring her tack and gun."

Baynes spoke to one of the cowhands, who went into the barn and emerged with Sam's things. When the hand had cinched the saddle and flopped down the stirrup, Lerner swung onto the roan, leaned toward the nearest of the rest of the horses, and fired into the air close by the animal's ear. The roan shied back a few steps against Lerner's hold, while the startled horse reared and bolted from the enclosure at a gallop, the others following.

Cavan studied Holt. "You are my meat."

"Yes he is," Baynes said to Cavan. "And I will pay you to take his life. Only now, do as he says."

"How much?" Cavan said.

Holt hated listening to men barter his murder. Before he could act, Lerner said, "Screw this," and fired again.

Cavan's holster tore. Lerner took two steps toward him. "Move!" he snapped.

For the moment Cavan was a believer. He went to the center of the yard, gestured for his men to gather close.

Holt put more pressure on Baynes's arm, and the old man moaned as Holt backed him away and out of the circle of the lanterns' glare.

CHAPTER
NINETEEN

It took them a while to reach the horses, which were picketed far enough away so no random nicker would reach Baynes's barnyard. Lerner had to mostly walk backward to keep an eye on Cavan and his mob, while Baynes was in no shape for this sort of nocturnal constitutional. "Cavan is a man for whom money talks," Lerner remarked to Baynes at one point.

Baynes was breathing too hard for conversation, and when they reached the horses, he sat heavily on a boulder and dropped his head between his knees. "I won't be dissuaded," Baynes said. "I'll see those heathens removed."

The clouds had broken somewhat, and in the starlight Baynes's wan face looked green. Lerner studied the elder with distaste, as if he were still a doctor and had just come upon a heretofore unknown type of tumor. "So that's what this is about," he said.

"A garden-variety anti-Semite," Sam said.

Baynes looked up. "I am obsessed."

"Indeed you are," Lerner said, "and I mean that in a clinical sense."

"I will not give up." Baynes rose to his feet; it cost him some effort. "Kill me now or die later."

"Let's get out of here," Sam said.

"My thought exactly," Holt said. "Cavan is bound to catch those horses sometime, plus I crave sleep."

Lerner pointed his gun at Baynes. "Sit down." When Baynes did, Lerner cocked the weapon and said, "I could do it, I think," as if speaking to himself.

Though his voice was calm, almost neutral, it made the skin at the small of Holt's back crawl. "What's this?" he said.

"The fancy man in Newport." Lerner was speaking to Holt but staring at Baynes. "He meant to kill me over a woman. Buddy back there, he was about to shoot you dead, same reason."

Now he was addressing Baynes. "Funny how easy it seems, once you've done two."

"No." To Holt's surprise, it was Sarah who spoke.

Lerner might not have heard. "Cut off the head and the snake dies," he said lethally.

At Holt's side, Sam stiffened. Like him, she saw that Lerner was considering this as a serious proposition. Sarah moved between Baynes and Lerner. Baynes looked away from her. Holt realized he was palming his own weapon, and wondered whom he meant to shoot.

"There must be a difference between him and us," Sarah said. "A person picks savagery or civilization, and this sorry, addled old man has chosen the former." She touched Lerner's gun. "Which will you choose?"

Under the pressure of her hand, Lerner's weapon slowly lowered. He returned it to leather, his expression sourly impotent.

"No one of you can do it, then," Baynes sneered.

"In another world," Lerner said, "you would be a goner."

"We live in this world." Baynes rose again and turned his back to them, started unsteadily toward the men a mile distant, who still stood knotted in a group under the lanterns' glare.

"Can we please get the hell back to Golem?" Holt said, supplicating. "I am full up to my craw with this philosophizing."

Lerner watched Baynes's back. "There remains the matter of the cattle drive to Provo." Lerner climbed onto his horse. "You will come."

"Not in this lifetime," Holt snapped.

Sam was staring at him, her lips curled in a faint smile.

"I guess we will," she said. "I've always wished to try droving."

"Why?"

"The quintessential romance of the West?" she suggested.

"You got a way of speaking that can rankle a man," Holt observed.

"I'm sorry," she said sincerely. "I was scared all the time I was with Baynes, and I'm not over it yet. I owe you, Holt. I knew you'd come, but I wasn't sure you could pull it off."

"I appreciate your confidence." They crested the pass and approached part of the trail that was flanked by drop-off. It was worse going down than coming up. It struck Holt as the perfectly dismal coda to this dismal day.

"I owe you all." She turned to Sarah. "To liberate me, you exposed yourself," Sam said. "I mean more than your body. He could have beaten you."

Sarah smiled at Holt. "You would not have let it happen."

"And that's the second reason we're going on that drive," Sam said to him. "If we do not, Cavan will prey, and you won't let that happen, either."

There was a difference, it occurred to Holt, between being in charge and being in control.

"Third is Gutt," Sam continued. "He might be drawn to us as well."

"Gutt is long gone," Holt said. Sam listened as Holt related his conversation with the Big Man that afternoon. It took his mind off his vertigo, at least. The drop-off seemed steeper in the dark. "If seeking Gutt is what this is about, we must do it elsewhere."

"We will," Sam said in his ear. "After we have helped these people."

The trail widened and Sam spurred her roan past him. "I suppose we will," Holt muttered.

* * *

The full-length door that backed up the bat wings at the saloon's entrance was padlocked, but Lerner produced a key. "Why am I not surprised?" Holt asked rhetorically.

Lerner lit a lantern. "Let's have a nightcap," he suggested. Holt realized that he'd scented no gin on Lerner since the man accosted him, nor observed evidence of drink's effect. He'd surely used his gun with a sober hand; apparently he could turn it on and off like others might work a pump handle.

Lerner was behind the bar splashing the liquor into a shot glass from which rose the familiar juniper aroma. "We'll need to sleep soundly." He tossed the shot down the hatch.

"I'll sleep like a dead man," Holt said.

"Poor choice of metaphor," Sam said. "We'll have one drink for the road. I'll make the cigarettes."

Holt handed her the pouch and accepted the bourbon that Lerner pushed toward him. "What'll it be, ladies?" Lerner asked.

Sam said she'd have a bourbon as well, concentrating on her smoke-building, while Sarah opted for water. Lerner poured, refilling his glass lastly and watching Holt over the brim.

Holt glanced at Sam. "We're going along," he said grudgingly. "Not that there's any guarantee we'll make it." He accepted a cigarette from Sam. "Fact is," Holt said, "I'd rate our chances poorly."

Sarah's hand had edged along the bar to pluck at the cloth of his sleeve. He pulled away. "It's eight of us against Cavan and his four remaining boys," Holt said. "But we've already seen what sort of shootists your three men are, and—"

"Don't say it," Sam cut in. She stared at Sarah, who nodded and said, "I'll need a gun."

"I'll rustle one up," Lerner offered.

"Cavan will follow," Holt insisted. "Baynes'll pay enough

to make it worth his while, even if Cavan didn't already want our hides out of pure meanness."

Lerner draped his hand over the neck of the gin bottle. "Go easy," Holt barked.

"I can hold it."

"Hold this," Holt went on angrily. "We can maybe get a few hours' head start, but the cows will make our pace no match for Cavan's." It wasn't pleasant to admit, but it had to be laid out on the table. "We'll be hunching our shoulders every moment of the day, wondering when a bullet is going to slice between them."

Lerner looked uncharacteristically solemn. He spoke quickly, in Hebrew. "What was that?" Holt demanded.

"A *broucha*," Lerner said, "invoking God's help."

"We'll need it." Holt pushed his glass away. "See you in the morning."

"Don't get too wedded to that pillow," Lerner said. "The cattle are gathered, and four would not be too early an hour to start."

Sam said her good-byes and went up the stairs. When she left, and then Lerner, Holt found himself alone with Sarah. The top two buttons of Lerner's borrowed shirt were undone, so Holt could see her breasts heave as she inhaled. "Well," she said.

"No." But she followed him up anyway, and to his back said, "Where will I sleep?"

The door of the next room down was unlocked, but when Holt threw it open, the kid Herschel sat bolt upright in the bed, blinked sleep from his eyes, and gave the two of them a salacious leer. "Find her a room," Holt snapped.

Herschel gazed at Sarah. "She could share this one."

Holt snorted, moved into the dimness and jerked Herschel from between the sheets. "Run along."

Herschel assayed Holt's mood, swallowed any smart rejoinder, and skedaddled. Holt was following him when Sarah said, "Why not?"

Holt forged ahead to his own room, closed the door and

leaned against it. "How the hell do I know?" he asked no one. "And how is it that I'm the one who is supposed to have all the answers?"

CHAPTER
TWENTY

For the next thirty-six hours, low-level dread rode close by Holt's head like an imaginary playmate. Above the saloon he slept badly, his dreams host to uninvited guests: Baynes, Cavan, the distorted Gutt, and lastly Sarah naked, the touch of her body so vivid that when a sharp rapping on the door awakened Holt, he was not surprised to see that she had snuck into his room after all and lay in his arms. He tried to tell himself he'd left the door unlocked by accident, but that was self-delusion, and as he came fully awake, it didn't matter anyway.

Lerner entered carrying a lantern, gazed at the two entangled forms in the bed, and had the sense not to say anything beyond "Time to head 'em up and move 'em out."

On a table downstairs was hot food from the café and the pretty waitress with a pot of coffee. If Sam knew or suspected that Sarah had come to Holt's bed, it wasn't nettling her.

For his part, Lerner must have been up for an hour already. After Holt visited the outhouse, he found the cattle gathered in the street before the saloon, three men circling them in the darkness and soothing the animals with low-voiced meaningless talk. The bay and roan and Sarah's horse were saddled, and at the rear of the herd, Mordecai Reich held the reins of a covered buckboard loaded with provisions, with four cows hitched as oxen.

Holt walked a gauntlet of townsfolk; the entire population must have turned out to see the drive off. The clouds had cleared completely by now, so starlight reflected the hope in their faces. As Holt tied his pack bags in place, Herschel plucked at his sleeve. "Don't get killed, okay?"

Holt looked at him. "Why not?"

"If you're dead, who's gonna teach me to shoot?"

The turnout of Golemites made Holt feel kindly. "You're a good kid, Herschel, but whatever happens, this is so long."

"I know." The kid was serious as well now. *"Sie gesund,"* he said.

"What's that mean?"

"Vaya con Dios, in Yiddish. I been studying a few of their words." Herschel grinned. "You take care."

Morris Levi, Ethan Cohen, and Noah Schwartz were quick studies on the trail, and by the end of the first day made pretty fair hands. Sam, too, was picking up the knack of turning a stray. They crossed water often enough to keep the cows content, and the first night camped by a stream with grass on the banks to provide a cud. Although they made, Holt reckoned, three miles each hour and pushed on until dark, the pace wasn't hard enough to take much flesh off the animals.

Reich cooked jerky stew and beans, and after the meal, the others insisted that Holt take no turn on the watch, having missed too much sleep already. It sounded like they'd discussed it aforehand behind his back. He acceded, but passed another night fitfully. If Cavan were to come, it would be under darkness's cover. But no ambuscade ruptured the desert's tranquility.

Now, at two in the afternoon on the second day, Holt's dread began to fade. He tried to keep a hook on it from the superstitious conviction that optimism was unlucky, but on a rational level he accepted for the first time that they might actually make it to Provo.

Cattle-driving was always ripe with the potential for catastrophe, but when it went smoothly, its mindless rote soothed a man. The weather remained clear, the streams ran low and were easy to ford this late in the season, and Holt's belly was full from the two sandwiches he'd eaten in the saddle. Reich made them after breakfast, diced jerked beef mixed with onions, on thick slabs of wheat bread smeared with mustard.

Holt rode drag; it was the best position from which to spot strays, and if Cavan attacked, it would most likely be at their backs. Lerner and Morris Levi were on one flank, Ethan Cohen and Noah Schwartz on the other, while Sam and Sarah led.

From the plank seat of the buckboard, Mordecai Reich said in his sonorous voice, "We may yet prevail, Mr. Holt," and Holt felt good enough to reply, "It could happen."

Later it would strike Holt that a man could do worse than abide superstition, because the remark seemed to undam a torrent of bad luck.

Holt was shredding the butt of a cigarette when Lerner dropped back to ride beside him. "Where are we?" Holt asked.

"More than halfway." They'd gotten moving before sunup again, and had another six hours ahead of them on this second day. "That's the good news," Lerner continued.

His tone brought the dread galloping back to Holt's side. "Meaning what?"

"Look yonder."

Before lunch Lerner had led them from the road and across trackless desert. Now Holt saw mountains maybe ten miles ahead, not like the hills separating Baynes from Golem, but the real McCoy; they rose four thousand feet above the desert floor if they rose a yard. Worse yet, Holt noted sourly, the sun sparkled off early snow glazing their peaks.

"That the only way to Provo?" Holt asked.

"No, but it's the fastest."

"Water?"

"There's a creek fifteen miles further on, but then not until the other side of the pass." Lerner gave Holt a weak smile. "After that it's downhill all the way to Provo."

"You left this part out. You might have asked my opinion."

"We'll camp at the creek," Lerner said, as if Holt had not spoken. "Tomorrow we cross over, and with luck we're in Provo before supper. I'll buy you a grilled pork chop."

Holt refused to be jollied. "First we've got to make it through the snow."

"Snow is water," Lerner said. "The cows can eat it."

Holt watched Levi chase and turn a stray. "You missed something in medical school, Doctor," Holt said. "The energy it takes to melt that snow in the belly will burn off flesh, the cows and ours."

"It's only one day," Lerner said.

Holt jerked the bay to a halt, so Lerner had to rein up to hear the rest. "I'm getting weary of you springing surprises," Holt said. "Don't do it again."

"Listen—"

"Go away," Holt said. When he turned his horse, he saw Reich auditing this exchange. Sam was riding back toward him, and Holt just knew she was bearing more bad tidings.

Her practice had not progressed to the point where she could roll without spilling. When the neck of her horse was sufficiently sprinkled with flakes of tobacco, Holt took the makings and did it for her.

"Tell me something," Sam said.

"I got the feeling it was about to be the other way around."

Sam lit the cigarette he gave her. "What sort of man is Clennon Pert?"

"Square enough, I suspect," Holt said. "There's a chance he is not a party to my predicament, except to the extent of doing his duty." He considered. "Same duty I did, until life went south on me."

"Baynes wired him as to our whereabouts," Sam said sheepishly.

Holt felt he'd been gut-kicked. "You judged it best to keep this to yourself?" he barked.

"I thought you had enough on your mind."

"Thanks very much." But Holt reined in his anger enough to listen to the rest of what she had learned from Baynes. "Don't keep secrets," he said when she was done. "That's the first rule, if we're going to have a chance of climbing out of the soup we're in."

Sam looked abashed. A heifer split from the herd, and as if in atonement, Sam broke away and headed it back where it belonged. Holt cantered after her. When she was finished, she turned her horse toward him again.

"All of what's happened," Sam said, "it seems plenty more right than wrong. Breaking you out of that prison, trying to find Gutt, and now this." She gestured to take in the bovines, moving along at a steady pace with heads lolling. "As to you and Sarah," Sam went on, "maybe I am a little jealous, and maybe it doesn't matter. What does matter is this."

Holt felt uncomfortable with her frankness.

"I'm with you," Sam said more firmly. "Through this drive, though whatever comes next, through to the time when you are cleared. Take it for what it is worth."

Sarah turned in her saddle to look back at them. She was smiling, as if she and Sam shared some secret.

"Whatever we have to face," Sam said to Holt, "it's good to know we'll face it together."

"That means a lot to me." Holt was surprised to find her

hand in his. He pulled back. "Facing trouble together is what partnering is about," he mumbled.

Sam laughed, but not in a way that gave offense. "You're some customer, Mr. Holt," she said.

CHAPTER
TWENTY-ONE

Rolling hills preceded the mountain range, and the desert gave way to meadow dotted with pockets of forest. With eight hours since the last water, and twilight coming on, the cattle were turning sluggish, but Holt knew they'd perk up when they scented the creek Lerner promised, which was not necessarily a good thing. In fact, as Holt rode up to Lerner on the flank, cattle raised their heads and sniffed at the air. "What goes on?" Lerner asked.

Once more the latter part of the day looked to bring a storm, but these clouds hung more darkly, and the air was flavored with a tart ozone taste. "They're fixing to run," Holt said in a low voice. "We can't afford to let them. They'll work off beef, and they'll be less fit for the climb tomorrow." Holt thought. "Who's your best man?"

"Levi."

Holt continued on to Sam and Sarah, told them to stay the hell out of the way in case of trouble, and sent them back to the left flank with Lerner and Cohen. Easing carefully around the herd, Holt moved Levi up to replace the women and put Schwartz on the flank with the others, taking the right point himself. There was no need for anyone on drag now; the cows weren't going in that direction. Holt gave the orders in a careful, quiet, neutral voice: no cigarettes, no noise, and if the cattle broke, the turn was to the right toward him.

The animals trudged on until they crested the last hill. At its base was the line of cottonwoods and willow thicket that marked the creek, about three-quarters of a mile distant.

168 When the sky flashed, and the top of the tallest cottonwood exploded in splinters. The bay's nostrils flared. Two seconds later the thunder boom of the lightning's strike reached them.

It did the trick. The lead cattle bellowed and bolted, and within moments the entire herd was on the stampede.

Levi did know what he was about. He had read the lightning well as Holt and moved a little left, and now he was in position to ride straight at the leaders, firing his handgun in the air to turn them.

Panicked, the first few cattle ducked contrarily to the left behind Levi's horse and away from Holt instead of toward him. His own gun was pointed skyward, but firing would have only harried them on—toward the left flankers, including Sam and Sarah.

The oxen yoked to Reich's wagon, eager to join the madness, bolted so suddenly the front wheels lifted. Reich jerked on the harness straps, but the buckboard was already careening off under his hand.

Holt raked at the bay with his spurs, but the horse would not enter the plunging herd, and Holt did not much blame him. He turned instead and galloped around the back end of the melee. Dust rose to mix with the rank smell of cow sweat and ozone.

Holt was halfway to heading them when thunder boomed again. Sam's horse whinnied and reared, and Sam tumbled from the saddle. The cattle bore down on her, the first animal ten yards away and closing fast.

Holt reined up, clutched hard with his thighs to keep his seat, jerked the Winchester from its sheath. He sighted, held a short breath, and fired.

A red hole appeared between the lead cow's eyes, and yet the contrary beast kept coming directly at Sam. Holt worked the rifle's lever and a shell casing flew away from him.

Before he could fire again, the animal stumbled, twisted, and went down, its bulk landing inches from Sam's head.

For a fraction of a second she did not move, and Holt

feared she had broken her skull or spine in the fall, but then she scrambled on hands and knees and drew her legs to her chest to make herself small behind the torso of the dead cow.

Animals veered and thundered past, their hooves striking up dirt all around her as they came in Holt's direction. Now he did fire, into the air, and by the mercy of God, they turned back toward Lerner and the other men.

The cowhands whooped and waved their hats, and by and by the cows began to circle. Holt walked the bay carefully through them as Sam got gingerly to her feet. Lerner had caught her roan and was leading it toward them as Holt reached her. "Are you all right?"

Sam brushed herself off. "Yes. Thanks again."

"They'll be okay now," Holt said. "They've got it out of their system."

Lerner dismounted to hand Sam the roan's reins, then drew a knife from his belt. The cow that Holt had shot was brain dead but still twitching. Lerner slit its throat and the animal lay still. Reich had the oxen team under control, and drove up to them. "There'll be fresh beef for supper," he said.

"Is a bullet-killed cow kosher?" Sam said.

Lerner spilled the animal's guts and started to skin the rib portion in preparation for cutting steaks. Reich nodded in satisfaction at his work and intoned, "Waste not, want not."

True to Holt's prediction, the cattle behaved themselves the rest of the way to the creek. The lightning bolt that struck the cottonwood had started a small fire, but the tree burned itself out before the flames could spread. Holt started his dinner famished; Reich had new potatoes to go with the beef, and the rabbi was a skilled hand with meat and fire. A pound and a half of T-bone steak later, Holt felt sated.

"I'll take a watch tonight," he announced. "Whoever is penultimate can wake me at three."

None of Lerner's men looked at him. To the ground, Levi said, "We've been talking."

Ethan Cohen said, "We are of one mind."

Reich had served himself last and was only halfway through his meal, but he set it aside and gave the three men his hard gaze. "Enough."

"What's going on?" Holt demanded.

"Melancholia and capitulation," Lerner said, also glaring at the men. "Common afflictions of our people."

The last of daylight faded to leave darkness framing the circle the eight of them formed around the fire ring. "Cavan is out there now," Schwartz said. "If he attacks . . ."

"We fight," Holt declared.

"I will not murder a man."

Before Holt could reply, another voice said, "That's good to hear."

Holt grabbed for his gun and he turned, but he was already covered by a Remington twin-barrel. The muzzle holes of the shotgun looked large as silver dollars. Holt raised his hands.

"That's the boy." The shotgun held steady. "There is an appetizing aroma in the air."

One steak remained on the grill. Holt said, "Rabbi, set a plate, please." Reich eased forward to do so; everyone else kept their hands well in sight.

"Murder is against the law," the shotgun wielder said.

"I've murdered no one," Holt said levelly.

Reich offered the steak. The newcomer considered the shotgun, finally propped it against the wheel of the buckboard but kept his hand on the barrel. "Anyone plan to murder me?" he asked.

Sam shifted. "That depends," she said dangerously.

The man wore a serge coat; he lifted the lapel to reveal a golden badge. "What it depends on," he said, "is whether you want to hang for the death of an official representative of the U.S. government."

"I was kidding," Sam said.

He cocked his head at her. "I suppose, like Mr. Holt, you

are innocent as well. You didn't bust anyone out of the
hoosegow."

"Would you by chance be Marshal Clennon Pert?" Sam
inquired.

Pert bowed more deeply. "The same, ma'am." Pert took
the plate and lifted it under his nose, inhaled deeply.

"My stars and garters," he said reverently. "Don't that
look like a bellyful."

Pert wore pants that matched his coat, and a four-in-hand
tie above a clean white shirt with ruffles alongside the buttons. He was a compact man of maybe fifty summers, but
fit and trim, his face unmarred by pox or liver spots. From
the front pocket of his shirt he took an ivory toothpick and
went to work on a sliver of gristle between his front teeth.
"Every being has something he can't do without," he said.
"For me, the toothpick is man's greatest invention."

Sam flicked her cigarette. "Marshal Pert?"

"Yes, ma'am?"

"You are on the track of the wrong man."

"That wouldn't surprise me." That gave Holt a ray of
hope that was instantly extinguished. "However," Pert continued, "I am dogged."

"Who framed me?" Holt demanded. "Fitzsimmons,
Stringer, or you?"

"The law says you killed that trollop," Pert went on,
"and I am the law's handmaiden."

"You don't understand a damned thing," Sam said.

Pert worked the toothpick as if he were digging for gold.
"You will see the cold steel bars of a cell as well," Pert
said. "Aiding and abetting."

"Here is a man who lives in his own world." This scene
struck Holt as surreal.

Reich had been at the wagon's back, scrubbing dishes in
a bucket of creek water, and now appeared with a handgun
pointed in Pert's direction, a Civil War–era horse pistol.
"Put them up," he said.

"For Jesus' sake," Holt said in disgust. He rose and took

the weapon from Reich, threw it back in the wagon. "Everyone settle down. Me and the marshal are going to make medicine."

Pert smoked the cigarette Holt made for him and listened patiently while Holt told his version of the murder of Cat Lacey, including his recent interview with Gutt. Holt went on to explain about Baynes, Cavan, and the threat he and his thugs presented at the moment.

When Holt was finished, Pert said, "They considered attacking you tonight, but I dissuaded them."

"What are you on about?" Holt snapped.

"I anticipated spending the night in your camp," Pert said. "Even a mobster like Cavan will not chance killing a lawman."

Pert tossed the butt of his cigarette into the fire. "I arrived at Mr. Baynes's spread about noon yesterday. By then Baynes suspected you had set out, and sent one of his cowhands to Golem. Indeed, the animals had departed, and it was a fair bet you were with them."

"I assume he omitted Cavan from his story," Sarah guessed.

"Yes, but I can follow a trail. The signs of your drive were clear, as were the signs of a band following you." Pert burped contentedly. "I perceived criminal activity in the making."

"We must succeed," Reich said.

Pert remained detached. "I snuck upon them and forestalled any ambush this night, as I told you. I know how to deal with Cavan's sort. Still, there is no law against riding the trail."

"Cavan is sworn to kill me," Holt said, "and Sarah as well."

"He beat me," Sarah put in.

Pert's eyes showed he knew she meant Baynes. "That grieves me, ma'am," he said. "I did not cotton to the man myself, but that cannot color the situation. I am the law."

"There is the law," Reich declaimed, "and there is God's righteous will."

"I'm concerned with the former," Pert said.

"That herd of cows—"

"Herd of cows?" Pert said. "Of course I've heard of cows."

That sunk it, far as Holt was concerned. He made his move.

Pert dropped his plate, rolled, and came up with the shotgun before Holt could clear leather. "You won't shoot me," Holt said.

"Probably not for having no sense of humor," Pert waved the double-barrel in a lethal gesture. "But you never know."

Sam stepped between them. "These people need us. You don't want to see them slaughtered by Baynes's thugs."

Pert took his time regarding her. "Aren't you the ball of fire." He stood, keeping the shotgun pointed at the ground.

Sam started to draw.

"Stop it," Holt said. "I'll take your gun if I have to."

"I wonder why I didn't think of that," Pert said. "Sounds like a good idea, now you mention it. Maybe you'd all best hand over your weapons to my custody."

Holt was hardly ready to fall for the notion that disarming them had only now occurred to the marshal. Behind the flowery rambling talk, Holt was certain, was one sharp, savvy lawman. "We might need them against Cavan. You've already figured that out."

"I told you he will not chance killing me," Pert insisted. "And tomorrow you and I and the lady will be long gone."

Holt sighed. "Listen up, Mr. Pert," he said. "My hunch is, first of all, that you had nothing to do with framing me for Cat Lacey's murder. My man is Fitzsimmons or Stringer."

"If you're speaking true."

"Second," Holt went on, "I think you believe me, but I also think you're not much concerned with justice."

"I do my job. You are a wanted man."

"Yeah, and we're worth five thousand dollars," Sam said.

"I am eligible for no reward, miss. By act of the U.S. Congress, my pay is sixty-five dollars per month."

"Third," Holt went on, "the way you came on in here against superior odds tells me you know some things and guessed others—such as that no one would molest you."

"Fourth," Sam put in, "you've saved us from Cavan, at least for the time being."

"I was thinking of my own skin," Pert contradicted.

"You are a curious man, Pert," Holt said, "in both senses of the word. You came to listen, and you've listened well. Now, there is one more thing you must know."

A cow lowed for the sake of hearing its own voice.

"I don't believe you are principally concerned with what Cavan might do," Holt continued, "but maybe you should be. You've got the power to condemn five men, and ruin a couple hundred other people, including innocent women and children."

"Innocence seems much on your mind this night, Mr. Holt," Pert said gravely.

"You know what I mean. If you take Sam and me, Cavan will know. Could be one of his boys is spying us out right now. I've told you how Baynes must stop this drive if he is to gain Golem."

Pert regarded him neutrally.

"Even if you take us tonight," Holt argued, "Cavan is only going to be cowed so much by the gold shield on your coat. I say he will shoot you from ambush, and then us, and cash us in for the reward. No one will know what became of our carcasses. His boys won't talk."

Pert pursed his lips. "What is your proposition?"

"Let us see the drive through to Provo," Holt said.

Pert took his time before nodding. "I will ride along, but once the cows are to market, I'm bound and determined to take you in."

"We'll deal with that when the time comes," Sam said.

"You can bet money on that, Miss." Pert got to his feet, went to his horse, retrieved his bedroll, and flopped it out. "You gonna shoot me in my sleep?" he inquired.

Sam actually smiled. "I suppose not."

"That's good to know." Pert returned to his horse. He uncinched the saddle and set it out for a pillow, burrowed deep into the blankets. "I'll see you all in the morning," he added. "Won't I."

In moment he was snoring something terrible. Despite the grass and water, it was almost loud enough to spook the cows once again.

CHAPTER
TWENTY-TWO

Holt's sleep was no less troubled that night, and he felt bearish when Lerner awakened him at three in the morning to serve his watch. Reich got up a half hour later and set to cooking. With the clouds gone, the night was chill enough to keep what was left of the butchered cow from turning rank, and at four the others arose to breakfast on more steak. A half hour later they mounted up and drove the cows across the creek, and by dawn were headed up toward the pass. The animals went reluctantly, as if they sensed they were heading for a bad end.

Holt felt about the same way.

The light of the rising sun was watery as the gulch narrowed, and the season changed with altitude from summer to bright autumn. The cattle labored, their vaporous breath the tangible representation of meat being worked off. The pass remained a goodly climb distant when the first patches of snow appeared on the sheltered side of the ravine. Soon after, drifts covered portions of the trail.

Pert rode back to Holt's drag position. "This is going to slow us," Holt observed.

"I reckon that's what our friends figure."

Holt turned in the saddle. About a mile back he made out five riders. "Could be they are merely dogging us," Holt said.

"Could be we will be compelled to fight for our lives," Pert suggested calmly. He looked upgulch. "Another five hundred feet vertical," he estimated.

Now the lead cows were shuffling through six inches of snow, and the sun was high enough to turn it wet and heavy. As it grew deeper the animals balked, and Lerner and his men were compelled to hurrah them on. The cattle looped and plunged, so steamy now that they produced their own cloud.

Holt looked back. Cavan and his men were closing on them. "He intends a confrontation," Pert said. "I feel it in my bones. They are old bones, and do not lie."

"So?"

"We push hard as we are able," Pert said.

"The way those cows are laboring," Holt said, "you can see the flesh melting away."

"You sound like a one-time cowman."

"I've been this and that," Holt said. "But never a killer."

"You've got a one-track mind, son. Concentrate on the business at hand."

But concentration eluded Holt. The cows ahead and the men behind divided his attention, and Holt found himself impatient, driving hard despite the cost in meat. With the pass no more than two hundred yards distant, the snow was shin deep to the animals, and they were struggling mightily.

As the head of the herd crested the pass, a crash sounded behind Holt. He spun in the saddle.

Reich had driven too close to a lodgepole pine and one side of the covered buckboard had plunged into the well of snow at its base. The wagon was propped against the tree at a forty-five-degree angle, the raised wheels spinning lazily. The torque of the accident had severed the wagon tongue, and the four oxen tried to bolt, but the snow and the yoke's weight hindered them and they gave it up.

Reich lay sprawled on his back in a supplicant position. Holt dismounted and waded to him.

Reich's eyes were open. "God has decreed to me Moses' fate." Reich did not move. "I shall not see the promised land."

Pert was at Holt's side. "We haven't time to right the wagon," Holt said to Reich. "You can ride double with me."

"I don't think so, son," Pert said gently. "He's hurt bad inside."

The marshal was right; when Reich spoke again, blood bubbled between his lips. "The brake lever struck me in the stomach." Reich tried and failed to sit. "Leave me," he said, "but fetch my gun."

Pert got it from the wagon's box, placed it in Reich's palm and wrapped his fingers around the grips. "It will be a comfort," Pert said, almost tenderly, but then looked over his shoulder and ordered, "Keep them moving."

"I will try to take one of them with me," Reich said. Pert placed a hand on Holt's shoulder and drew him away. Holt felt reluctant and helpless. He gathered up the bay's reins and was swinging into the saddle when the rifle shot rang out.

The noise came from ahead and to the right. Holt glanced back. Where Cavan and his four men had been, only two remained, within five hundred feet of their position. Holt looked about, found Cavan horseback a little on the slope of the ridge line, a hundred feet distant and fifty above, with a rifle aimed dead-on at him. "Right now, next few seconds," Cavan called, "there could be a massacre. You want to see that happen, Marshal?"

"Not especially," Pert hollered back.

Cavan rode closer and Holt could make out his smile. Cavan's other two boys backed him. "Everyone hold tight," Cavan said, "and we will have done with our business."

The clear, thin, sunlit air magnified distance. From the top of the pass, Holt could see, at least ten miles distant on the flat below, the settlement of Provo. Streaking toward the horizon from the north end of town, straight as a ruler line across the desert floor, was the railroad to Salt Lake, the path of salvation for the people of Golem and their beef.

Holt wondered if he'd ever reach it.

"I am riding in," Cavan announced. He proceeded down the slope toward Holt.

Behind Holt another gun went off.

"Don't draw," Pert snapped. Holt took his hand from his gun butt and turned slowly. By the wagon, Cavan's men held drawn guns, but the powder smoke that drifted on the air came from Reich's weapon, and its barrel was in his mouth.

"He drew on us," one of the men called, shifting his gaze from Pert to Cavan and back again, "but we didn't shoot no one, Mr. Marshal. You can see he done himself."

Pert was at the back of the herd, Lerner and his three boys on the flank, and Sam and Sarah watched this from the head end. Cavan rode to within a half-dozen yards of Holt, the rifle steady.

"Do you know me, Marshal Pert?" Cavan asked, staring at Holt. "I gave you my name."

"And I have been pondering on it." Pert pursed his lips. "You are the egg-sucking bastard who shot a lawman in Durango."

"I was tried for such a crime," Cavan said, "and found innocent. There is no paper on me."

"There will be," Pert warned, "if you commit violence this day."

Cavan shook his head. He wore only a shirt and vest beneath his trademark derby. "This will be a fair fight, Marshal."

Cavan sheathed the rifle while keeping his free hand close to his sidearm. He dismounted, smiling broadly.

"You see, Marshal," he said, "this Holt hombre is going to call me out."

Cavan ordered Holt's group off their horses, then had them drop their guns in a pile and stand close together for easier watching. While they complied, he stood splay-legged and shin deep in the wet snow, oblivious to its cold.

Pert said, "I charge you with intimidation, rustling, and whatever else I can think of by and by."

Cavan laughed. "Here is a real-life situation, Marshal, and no crime to be committed. I offer a deal, and a better one than I might, given the circumstances." While he speechified he kept his gaze on Holt, who faced him at ten paces.

"These men," Cavan went on, meaning Lerner's three cowhands, "they have no stomach for gunfighting. This means that if they begin such a fight, they will die. Facts is facts."

Levi, Cohen, and Schwartz looked sheepishly at the snowbound ground. It was affirmation enough.

"This I propose," Cavan said. "No matter how I fare in this set-to, I will allow you free passage."

"You won't do Baynes's bidding?" Sam asked.

Cavan combined Baynes's name with an obscenity. "I will take my profit from you, missy, and this bastard's carcass."

"That's murder all the same," Pert put in.

"Not in any court hereabouts. Fair fight," Cavan insisted.

Mania brightened his eyes. Holt would have admitted it to any man who asked: He was scared as he'd ever been in his life, because there was another admission bubbling to be shared.

He'd never been in a head-to-head gunfight.

"We finish this now," Cavan said.

Nor did Holt believe Cavan would—or could—keep his word. "Your men don't look the type to let five thousand dollars waltz on down the trail," Holt said. "The moment I kill you, they will open fire."

Cavan laughed and snapped his fingers. "Billy and Ray," he said. "Come forward."

The two men behind him frowned at each other. "What's this?" the one called Billy said.

Cavan spun as he drew, moving as fluidly in the deep snow as if it were air. He fired and Billy's hat flew away.

Holt felt weak.

"Do as you are told," Cavan said. When the men approached, he went on, "I'll have your guns."

Cavan holstered his own to take the weapons from them. He nodded to the other two and similarly ordered them to disarm. "Jack there is Billy's brother, and Frank . . ." Cavan smiled at Frank. "Frank has got a special regard for Ray," he finished nastily.

"You're a little insane, son," Pert commented.

"My professional opinion, I agree," Lerner put in.

"Come forward, Mr. Liveryman," Cavan said. Cavan set his men's guns on the snow's crust close by Lerner. "I have seen your shootist skills," Cavan said. "If the result does not go my way, you will be able to snatch up a weapon and forestall any predation." Cavan waggled his handgun in Lerner's face. "Not before, though."

"You'll get us all killed," Billy said.

Cavan studied Holt. "Only one man dies today," he declared. He glanced at Pert. "This all right with you, Marshal?"

"Absolutely not," Pert said.

Cavan took in the stolid herd of cattle, the field of snow in which they stood, the mountains that were proscenium to this drama. Lastly he turned his gaze back to Holt, favored him with a smile bright as the glary light.

"Is this not a pretty day for a gunfight?" Cavan asked.

Holt worked to tamp down his fear as he faced Cavan. "You will do it?" he said. "You will let the drive proceed?"

"I gave my word." Cavan's hand hovered above his gun butt. "As I gave my word to kill you and have your woman." Cavan approached to within five paces.

"Draw well, son," Pert cautioned.

That struck Holt as a huge help. "You take pleasure from this," he said to Cavan.

"Enough talk. Slap leather."

Holt did, before the sentence was complete—

And saw in an eye blink what was about to happen.

He dropped toward the snow as his barrel cleared the holster.

Cavan shot him.

One of the women screamed as Holt went down with a bolt of pain searing through his left side. Another gun fired. Holt caught a peripheral view of one of Cavan's men tumbling snowward.

Cavan lined on Holt, holding his gun two-handed. The woman screamed again. "Stay very still," Cavan said. From the corner of his mouth he said, "I forgot about Ray's sneak gun. Who was he fixing to shoot, you or me?"

"Hard to say," Lerner replied.

"Ray didn't cotton to my byplay," Cavan said, "but neither was he much of a one for brains."

The pain in Holt's side was wondrously brilliant, and he felt within seconds of passing out.

"Set that rifle back down," Cavan told Lerner. "There ain't no more sneak guns hereabouts."

Lerner gave up the weapon. Pert said, "You kill him now, it will be murder after all."

"I'll take him the way he is," Cavan said. "Likely he'll die on the trail."

Though his hand was still on his gun, Holt reckoned Cavan was right. If he lost consciousness now, he'd never wake up.

Holt raised his revolver and Cavan let him, his own gun up and his ugly grin behind the sights.

A shot sounded, punier than the others. Holt rolled onto his back and over to his stomach again. Cavan fired and missed him by inches. Blood stained the middle of Cavan's shirt.

Holt used it as a target and shot him three times. A lot more blood spurted onto the snow as Cavan threw up his hands. The gun arced away and Cavan went down on his back and lay still.

On the shots' echo, no one moved. Then Pert advanced cautiously and touched Cavan's neck. "He's done," he announced.

Lerner covered Cavan's remaining three boys with one of their own rifles.

Pert came to Holt, removing his neckerchief. He wiped sweat from Holt's forehead, the gesture oddly tender, and held his hand out to show Holt a one-shot derringer smaller than the marshal's palm. "Cavan was wrong," Pert said. "Turned out there was another sneak gun after all."

Lerner crouched by Holt. "Best thing, Marshal," Lerner said, "would be for you and the boys to tear enough planks from that wagon yonder so I can get him off the snow, and extra to build a fire. Cut up some of the cover for a blanket and bandages, if you'd be so kind."

Sam knelt in the snow to take Holt's hand. "You'll be okay," she said.

"Jesus God," Holt muttered. "I hate getting shot."

Holt didn't pass out after all, and after cutting away enough of his shirt to see the wound, Lerner seconded Sam's prediction. He covered Holt with his own jacket and produced a pint of gin from his saddlebag. "Drink fast as you can get it down. You'll be in some pain in a little while."

"I'm in pain now." Holt's shirt was wet with blood, but Lerner kept pressure on the wound, and the flow slowed while they waited for the jerry-rigged bed to be made and a fire built.

Cavan's boys were sullenly following Pert's order to help out. When the job was done, Pert said, "Thanks, lads. You'll be moving on now."

"What about our guns?" Frank demanded.

"They're in my custody for the nonce," Pert said.

"That's thievery."

Holt laughed, wondered if he was turning delirious.

"You can pick them up at the office of whatever law they got in Provo," Pert said, "but not before the day after to-morrow."

Frank squatted by Ray's body. "What if we run into a griz?"

"For that to happen, you'd have to grow angel wings and fly to the Yellowstone country," Pert said, "because that's where the nearest griz is."

"He ought to have a burial."

"Ground's frozen," Pert observed. "You'll have to take him with you." Pert cleared his throat delicately. "I know how you feel, son."

"In a pig's valise." Frank spat and stood, pointed at Lerner. "That hombre shot him down."

"I rule it self-defense," Pert said.

"And you plinked Cavan while he wasn't looking. Good as back-shooting the poor bastard."

"You didn't care for him, son," Pert said soothingly. "I doubt if anyone did, including his mother, if he had a mother."

"Someone has got to pay," Frank persisted. "Gimme a gun. I'm calling your goddamn sawbones out, just him and me."

"Move on, son."

Frank took a step. Lerner drew, nearly as quick as Cavan. "The marshal is saving your life, pal," Lerner said.

The other two had already mounted up. Frank looked up at them and said, "Gimme a hand with Ray."

One snorted; the other looked away. In the end it was Levi and Cohen who helped Frank get Ray draped over his saddle. Pert stared at their backs as they started down the southern slope. "I could almost feel sorry for that boy."

"You got too much compassion, Marshal." Lerner holstered his weapon. "Me, I got Mr. Holt here, getting my coat all bloody."

Holt lay bare to the waist on the pallet, but the fire was within arm's length and blazing. He sweated in its heat and from the pain, sharp enough despite the liquor to cause considerable misery. The kettle of water on the flames was boiling. Lerner dipped some out into a smaller cook pot and put it in the snow to cool.

A creaking sounded as Lerner's men got the wagon levered back onto its wheels. They went to work rebolting the tongue, and when that was done, loaded the bodies of Reich and Cavan onto the bed. A three-foot-wide puddle of blood covered the depression Cavan had made.

By then the water had cooled enough so Lerner could wash his hands. He sluiced what was left over Holt's wound.

Holt forced himself to look. The hole, luridly red-rimmed, was in his left side at the same latitude as his belly button.

"I'd guess it glanced off a rib," Lerner opined. "Likely cracked it, but that's not serious. You seeing double or thinking fabulous thoughts?"

"Yeah." Holt's voice slurred, and he waved the gin bottle. An inch remained. "Maybe this has something to do with it."

Sam crouched at the fire with her back to him. Holt either remembered or dreamed—he wasn't sure which—that he'd seen Lerner talking to her in confidential tones.

"You haven't expectorated blood," Lerner said. "Your insides remain unpunctured."

Without warning Lerner took the bottle and poured some of the gin into the hole. It felt like liquid fire and Holt screamed. Lerner rolled him over. "The bullet passed through cleanly. I don't see any fragments." Lerner's finger stabbed into the exit wound and Holt screamed again.

"Keep digging," he got out through clenched teeth. "You might strike ore."

More gin trickled into him. "Time to close up," Lerner said cheerfully. Sam moved from the fire.

She carried a knife, its blade glowing red.

"You traitor," Holt said thickly.

Holt thought by now that he knew pain like a best friend, but the cauterization was a torment like nothing Satan could have devised. Holt heard his flesh sizzle under the blade's sear, and this time, as hands rolled him over for a second application to his front, he could not release the scream from his throat, and in frustration and agony went away from there into blackness.

CHAPTER
TWENTY-THREE

Holt opened his eyes to stars shining through a flapping hole in canvas. When he raised his head, he discovered two horses ambling on tethers, Lerner's and his bay. That put him in the righted wagon, which was moving downhill.

His hand brushed something scratchy. He turned and his nose was inches from the bearded face of Reich's corpse, as if they were sharing a bed, and Cavan lay beyond the rabbi. Holt sat up too quickly. His head hurt as badly from the gin as his side did from the various insults, ballistic and medicinal, it had suffered. His rib cage was bound with canvas bandages pinned tight, and over it was a clean cotton shirt that was not his.

Holt got his hands and knees under him, unwadded his coat, which had been folded into a pillow, and crawled to the wagon's head end. Lerner was at the reins. "Go back to bed," he said.

"I sleep poorly among corpses." Holt settled beside Lerner and shrugged into the coat.

They were nearly on level ground, and the trees lining another creek were silhouetted by starlight maybe a mile ahead. "The cold was burning too much off the cows, and they need grass and a drink," Lerner said. "I decided we'd best move on."

Holt pulled his watch and held it close to his face: It was a few minutes after two, so he'd been out eight hours. He laughed and winced at the new pain it caused. "You were right," he said. "My rib is broke."

"You find that amusing?"

"I was thinking I had to get shot for a good night's sleep."

Pert rode up to the wagon. "How you feeling, son?"

"Like I been worked hard and put up wet. I suppose I'm okay."

"That's fine," Pert said.

"Live folks being easier to transport than corpses," Holt suggested. His gun belt had been removed for Lerner's treatment, and he was not surprised to see it, and Sam's, looped over Pert's saddle horn.

Pert rode along for a full minute without speaking. "Son," he said then, "I'm starting to like you."

Holt went to work on a cigarette.

"But that don't change the facts of life," Pert went on. "Like I said—"

"You are dogged," Holt finished for him.

"That's it in a nutshell," Pert said.

"Anyway," Holt said, "thanks for saving my hide."

"Seeing a helpless creature gunned sticks in my craw."

"Just how I like to picture myself," Holt said ironically. "Out of what thin air did your sneak gun appear?"

Pert rolled back his right sleeve. "I knew a peashooter like this wouldn't down him, but I figured it'd get his attention." The marshal reached up to show Holt a metal brace strapped by leather thongs on his forearm, with a rod running along the brace and ending in a clip that held the tiny pistol by the butt. Pert pressed at a catch near his elbow, and a spring released, dropping the gun into his hand and opening the clip.

"A pimp's getup," Pert said. "Kind of embarrassing, but an old man needs an edge. Don't be blabbing about it, okay?"

"You are one odd duck, Mr. Pert," Holt said. Pert nodded as if he had been complimented and went off to tend the animals. Holt blew smoke. "How far to Provo?"

"Two or three miles."

"Only another hour, then."

"We'll bargain better on a few hours sleep, and the cows

can feed and water," Lerner said. "We can afford the time, now that Cavan's taken care of."

Given what had happened so far, Holt wasn't about to call this drive a sure thing until it was over, but Lerner was right, and maybe he could use the time to figure some way to evade Pert.

The cattle were milling along the creek now, Levi keeping them away from the campsite. Lerner reined up. "We can drive them the rest of the way by ourselves," he said.

"Run out while Pert sleeps," Holt said. "That occurred to me."

It had also occurred to Pert; Holt should have figured it would. After Lerner drove the wagon across the creek to the campsite and Holt stepped down, Pert produced a pair of handcuffs. "If you've any business to do, go ahead and use them bushes," Pert said. "After that, I guess I got to hook you up to that wagon wheel. I need my forty winks."

Holt shook his head. "I've got too much to do. I can fix some breakfast; we'll need it when you've had your beauty sleep." Holt called Levi over. "I'll bury the rabbi," Holt volunteered, "if you want to say something over him before you turn in."

"That would mean a lot." With Cohen and Schwartz, Levi went to get Reich's body from the wagon.

"I'll plug Cavan as well," Holt said to Pert. "Unless you've grown accustomed to having him around."

The boys lay Reich upstream, on the other side of camp from the cows, in the soft dirt by the creek. Holt heard chanting in what he'd come to recognize as Hebrew.

"Also, someone has to watch the animals," Holt added.

Pert was pondering when Sam came to them, Sarah at her side. "I'm glad you're still alive," Sam said.

"Yeah, me too."

She surprised him by stepping inside his arm and planting a kiss on his cheek. Holt was thankful for the dark, because he could feel his face redden.

Pert cleared his throat. "I don't reckon you'd kill me

while I snooze. Or that you'd run out on this one," Pert grinned, "not now."

"Keep your nasty thoughts to yourself, Marshal," Sam said, but lightly.

"I'm a fool for romance." Pert took her hand and snapped one link of the cuffs over her wrist, the other on his own. "But for tonight, ma'am, it's you and me who're bunkmates."

Holt dug Cavan's grave behind the wagon, shallow and away from the water, and dumped the man in face first. It was a childish gesture, but dead was dead, and Holt remained a tad irritated that Cavan meant this burying to be the other way around.

He took a deal more care with Reich. A half foot down he struck wet clay, harder to dig but making for better aesthetics, and Holt took advantage, cutting the sides straight vertical and making the space extra long and wide to accommodate the rabbi's bulk. Dirty dawn appeared in the east, and with it and the exertion, Holt warmed enough to strip down to his union suit. By the time he was satisfied with his work, standing in the pit and leaning on the shovel handle, he was well muddied. Without available help, he was compelled to drag Reich's body by the feet and bump it sharply into the space, but the indignity couldn't be helped.

Despite his skepticism toward religion in general, Holt felt reverent at the moment. Reich had his faults, no least among them a mild case of the fervors. Also, Holt figured that as in most churches, Jews considered suicide a mortal sin. But Reich had done plenty for his people, and now it looked like his work would survive him. The dozing cows were going east to slaughter, and Golem was going on to prosperity.

And where are you going? Holt thought.

He patted down the mound of clay-bound dirt and stepped back to admire the job, but his mind was elsewhere. His gun, he had earlier noted, was stashed under the arm of the marshal where he lay tethered to Sam and snoring. But the cowhands had their arms back, and what would happen, Holt contemplated, if he were to borrow one and set the barrel against Pert's temple and wake him ever so gently and promise to blow his brains from here to Durango if he did not uncuff Sam and let them ride out.

Holt knew what would happen, and so did Pert, and that was why guns were available to him: Pert would call his bluff, and Pert would win, because the marshal would know he was not about to kill him, in cold blood or any other way.

Damn the man for his insight.

Holt thought: He could knock the marshal cold, bean him with the crowbar from the wagon's tool kit, and then use it to break the handcuffs' chain. Holt listened to the rush of the creek for several minutes before muttering some curse words. He went upstream a ways so his noise would awaken no one, stripped off the mud-smeared union suit and took it with him, not so much walking as marching into the water.

It fed from the mountains and was icily chill. Shivering, Holt washed first the underwear and then himself, fully immersing, as if the sting the water brought to his wound would shake the frustration out of him.

He was not going to coldcock the marshal, either, something else they both knew. His contrary will answered. *Then you will rot in a cell for the rest of your living days.*

Holt wrung the union suit and threw it over a cottonwood branch, then went back to where he had set his outer garments well away from the grave's mud. As he bent to pick them up, a deep, low, guttural voice said, "Hold like that."

Holt did as he was told, hunched over with gun-metal cold as the creek touching at the small of his naked back, his equipment swinging in the dawning light of day. He recognized the voice, and felt as bereft as he could ever remember.

* * *

Morning came quickly on the desert and had mostly arrived when Holt, still naked, followed the order to stop, a hundred yards up from the campsite. A train's air horn sounded from the direction of Provo, no farther than the next drainage.

"You can turn around."

Holt did, and said, " 'Morning, Mr. Gutt." Gutt held his gun in one hand and Holt's clothing in the other. He tossed him the latter.

"I thought we were done with each other for the time being," Holt said, balancing precariously as he got his legs into his britches.

Gutt threw him his boots. "You know what they say about Abraham Lincoln," Gutt said.

The Big Man's reappearance raised all sorts of disturbing and deadly questions, and Holt had been working to keep his fear under control since he'd heard the voice, but now it was replaced with a dizzying feeling that reminded him of his vertigo.

Gutt pointed at the canvas bandages around Holt's rib cage. "Did Cavan shoot you?"

"Yeah," Holt said pettishly, "and what do they say about Abraham Lincoln?"

"That this John Wilkes Booth was not acting alone," Gutt said. "They say he was an agent of General Lee, who meant by the President's death to turn the tide of the war."

Holt buttoned his borrowed shirt and put his vest on over it. Sunlight was hitting them directly now, and he did not need the coat.

"A conspiracy," Gutt said. "As I am caught up in."

"Where's my hat?" Holt demanded.

"You won't need it. I am compelled to kill you."

"Why not do it while I was naked? It seems fitting."

Gutt's massive head moved left to right. "I have killed many, but I've never embarrassed a man."

"I'm not embarrassed, goddamn it," Holt spat. "I'm scared and depressed and confused. I thought you said you weren't going to kill me, and what's this conspiracy business?"

Gutt gave Holt his awful gaze. "Baynes knows all."

"About the drive?" Holt nodded toward the milling cattle.

"About the woman." Gutt sighed; it sounded like a donkey wheezing. "Your Cat Lacey."

"How?"

Gutt shrugged. "He is a capitalist. The man who hired me was a capitalist."

That could mean either Fitzsimmons or Stringer, Holt thought, and was no big help.

"Capitalists stick together, like a conspiracy," Gutt said. "Now it is you or me."

"In what way?"

"If I don't kill you," Gutt said, "Baynes will air the truth of the matter. I believe he can make it stick. He will tell your Marshal Pert this very morning."

Gutt looked at the ground. "He sent a man to intercept me with this news. We left hours after Pert, riding hard. Now we are here. I do his bidding or I serve your time."

"Who is this 'we' you keep mentioning?"

"Me and Baynes."

"Where is he?"

Baynes stepped from the brush, holding a rifle and looking crazy as seven waltzing coyotes. "Right here, Mr. Holt," he said.

Gutt smelled like what was left of a gopher the day after a hawk had plucked away the tasty parts. Holt savored his rank odor from the vantage of Gutt's armpit, into which his head was jammed, while Gutt held a gun to his forehead.

"Disarm yourselves," Lemuel Baynes said, "or Holt dies."

Baynes sat horseback holding his rifle on the others, who were standing in a knot before the wagon. Pert had not had a chance to unshackle himself from Sam, and the wrist to which she was attached was Pert's right; so much for sneak guns, Holt thought. He ranked his chances of getting out of this on a par with being called to Salt Lake and appointed to the Council of Elders.

"You can't do this, Baynes," Pert said.

"But I must. I have no choice." Baynes seemed to be pleading his case, as if he could convince Pert—all of them—of the rightness of this moment.

"At all costs," Baynes went on, "Golem and its heathen citizenry must be destroyed, and that means you must be stopped. I sensed Cavan would fail, and I followed."

"Sensed how?"

Sarah's defiant tone only made Baynes smile. "The angel Moroni came to me."

"He makes house calls?" Lerner muttered.

Baynes raised the rifle, and Holt thought Lerner would be shot. Baynes continued over the sights. "You could have wandered the desert as your people were fated to do," he said. "Now you must die. It is the only way."

"If you touch any one of these folk," Pert said, "I will see that you hang."

"Not from the grave," Baynes said. He looked down at Gutt. "Release the murderer."

Gutt let Holt go, and while he was off balance, shoved him toward the others. Holt stumbled to his knees and felt new pain from his bullet wound.

"Very good," Baynes said, like a schoolteacher. "Stay down." He tossed the lever-action rifle and Gutt caught it.

"Holt first, and then the woman." Baynes drew his handgun and aimed it at Sarah. "Finish the rest, but leave my wife to my swift vengeance."

Gutt shifted the rifle's muzzle to home in on Holt. "As I spoke," he said, "it is you or I."

"You expect me to empathise?" Holt said hoarsely.

"Do what I told you!" Baynes ordered. "Bring down upon them the wrath of the Lord."

Gutt said to Holt, "Place your hands flat on the ground, palms down. If you don't, he says I must shoot."

Holt did it. Gutt stepped forward, now holding the rifle by the stock and barrel, raised vertically.

"I keep my promise," Baynes pronounced. "Your hands will be useless skin bags of shattered bone, and you will sit in a cell helpless as a child, while others have their pleasure with you." To Gutt he snapped, "Now! Crush them!"

Gutt did not move.

"Do it or I will kill you, you perverse monstrosity," Baynes fairly screamed. "I demand you fulfill my will."

Holt imagined the unendurable pain of a gun butt driven down with all Gutt's awesome strength. The hairs of his knuckles quivered.

Baynes turned his gun on Gutt. "Smash him and kill the rest, you cretinous grotesque abomination."

Gutt spun, crouched, and shot Baynes in the heart.

Baynes's eyes went wide with incredulity. He touched at his chest, stared at his blood-smeared palm, and tumbled backward in the saddle to crash to the ground. His foot tangled in the stirrup and his startled horse dragged him a few feet before coming to an uneasy halt. Gutt back-stepped, unloosed Baynes's foot from the stirrup, and let the leg drop heavily. Never taking his eyes from them, he swung into the saddle.

"Guess you'll be after me from here on," he said to Pert.

"The law's got something called justifiable homicide," Pert said, "but on the other hand, a jury's supposed to decide what's justifiable. This will take some thought."

"Then there's you," Gutt said to Holt. "From a practical point of view, that hand-crushing business had its advantages."

Gutt walked the horse backward. "Too late. For now," he said to all of them, "we are done." He faced them until he was out of range, then turned the horse and headed back up toward the pass.

"So he's the one you claim done the whoor?" Pert asked.

"That's right," Holt said.

Pert turned his gaze to Baynes's bleeding corpse. "Maybe so, maybe not," he said. "Right now it looks like there's more burying to be done."

CHAPTER
TWENTY-FOUR

The air horn sounded again, this time to warn not of the train's approach, but its departure. From its open stock cars wafted a rank smell that was nonetheless pleasant on Holt's nostrils, as it rose from Golem's hundred cows on their way to market. Golem was now better than a couple of thousand dollars richer; Lerner had negotiated from the broker a price of twenty-two dollars a head.

"You did a fine and charitable job, son," Pert said in Holt's ear. "Now I got to do mine."

Pert produced his steel bracelets, clamped them on Holt's wrists. Sam worked the pouch from Holt's pocket and began to make cigarettes. "Are you going to manacle me as well, Marshal?" She licked at the paper.

"Only got the one pair of cuffs," Pert admitted. "You mind rolling one for me?"

As the railroad's principal business involving this trunk line to Salt Lake was cattle, there was no station, only a maze of post-and-pole stockyards at the end of a five-fingered hand of dead-end sidings. Provo looked to be a crude town, although Holt had not had the chance to tour it firsthand. Pert had kept a tight leash on him since they'd successfully finished the drive.

Lerner turned from watching the train depart and came over. Levi, Cohen, and Schwartz were perched on the rails of one of the corrals. Levi had obtained a pint of dark liquor somewhere, and the three men were passing it among them. Holt could have used a taste.

"So you are taking these desperadoes in," Lerner said to Pert.

"I must do my duty," Pert replied. "I am—"

"Don't say it again," Holt interrupted. "Where are we headed?"

"Out of Utah for starters," Pert said. "I've had my fill of Mormon justice."

"Lots of things could happen trailwise," Holt observed.

"One never knows." Sam seemed almost gay, which struck Holt as odd considering that Pert was going to have his way.

"Might as well fill your belly before you leave," Lerner said. "I found a café that puts up a pretty fair bowl of chili."

"Trail is awaiting us." Pert considered. "On the other hand, I've always had a weakness for chili."

It struck Holt that he hadn't seen Sarah that morning. "I wouldn't mind saying good-bye to Miss Baynes," he said.

"Let's eat," Sam said.

Pert dug at the dirt with the toe of his riding boot. "Why not," he said.

The café was more rude than Golem's, and stunk only marginally less than the stockyards, from cowshit tracked in by workers' boots. But the nose got used to anything after a time, and Holt was hungry and in need of coffee. A middle-aged waitress poured him some, said, "Four chilis coming up," and went off to the kitchen.

Pert sat with his back to it, Holt facing him. Behind him Holt spotted Sarah in the kitchen with the waitress. To Holt's mystification, Sarah was giving the waitress money.

The waitress returned with heaping bowls of meat and beans, started to set out one in front of Holt. In the kitchen door Sarah cleared her throat loudly.

The waitress spun on her heel and gave the bowl to Pert instead. The waitress looked sheepish, but Pert was too busy leaning over to savor the aroma to notice. Food appeared to be the one thing that could occupy his full attention.

A half-dozen spoonfuls later, Pert clutched his gut and gasped, "My great-grandmother's aunt's fanny."

Holt assumed this passed as a swear term for the prim marshal. Pert doubled over, and while he was thus preoccupied, Lerner's hand dipped into his pocket. "The facilities," Pert muttered.

Sarah stepped up to the table, pointed toward the back door and said, "That way."

Pert bolted from the table like a quarter horse.

Sarah took Pert's vacated chair as Holt turned to Lerner. "If that was rat poison," Holt said, "I'm not sure you helped the situation."

"You know how doctors are always recommending 'a mild purgative'?" Lerner produced the key he had filched from Pert's pocket and unlocked Holt's handcuffs. "The one Sarah paid the waitress to put in his chili wasn't mild."

Lerner stowed away a big spoonful of the beans and meat. "He'll be spending some time in that outhouse," he said, "and it'll be a day before he can sit a horse. Still, I wouldn't tarry over breakfast."

Holt pushed his bowl away. "I lost my appetite."

"I had the boys saddle your horses and strap on your bags. You can keep the shirt."

"Thanks," Holt said. "I don't just mean for the shirt." He rose and they shook hands. "Good luck. Tell Herschel I asked after him."

Sarah rode with them to where the trail forked to the north a couple miles out of Provo. "I'll be heading on to Salt Lake, I suppose," Sarah said.

"You have people there?" Sam asked.

Sarah shook her head and took Holt's hand. He was trying to reckon whether he liked having his hand held—it sure seemed to be happening a lot lately—when Sarah released it. "No. From there I go east."

"You've got years to make a future," Sam said.

"As do you," Sarah said.

Sam looked about to grab his hand herself, but instead dug his makings from his shirt pocket. "We'll see," she said, looking at Sarah but talking, Holt would have sweared, to him.

"We could both get lucky," Sarah said. Sam rode her horse flank to flank with Sarah's and the two women hugged.

Holt coughed.

Sam looked at him, vastly amused. "Frog in your throat?" she inquired.

"Time to ride," Holt said. He pointed the bay west, and Sam fell into place at his side.